AF593314

Double Vision

Double Vision

GILLI WRIGHT

Hamish Hamilton · London

For Becky,
and for Ben, who gave me Jessica

First published in Great Britain 1986 by
Hamish Hamilton Children's Books
27 Wrights Lane London W8 5TZ

British Library Cataloguing in Publication Data
Wright, Gilli
Double Vision
I. Title
823'.914 [J] PZ7
ISBN 0-241-11996-0

Typeset by Katerprint Typesetting Services, Oxford
Printed in Great Britain by
Butler & Tanner Ltd, Frome and London

One

Sam rubbed his sleeve against the steamed-up window pane and peered through his peephole down on to the court between the tower blocks. Warm as he was, he could see that it was a cold day out there. A blue car edging round the court seemed to be pursued by its own personal cloud, as the heat of its exhaust clashed with the air. The squat figure of a woman in a bobble hat and maroon coat, pushing a toddler in a chair, swelled out in front so conspicuously that Sam was alarmed for her. Shouldn't she be in the hospital? What if she had the baby right there in the court? It would rocket out and fall on its head on the concrete. She turned to wave at someone and Sam saw with relief that her loose coat flattened against her stomach; it was nothing but air. The worn patch of grass in the centre of the court still bore a faint trace of frost.

The hurrying figures vanished behind one or other of the tower blocks and the court was empty, save for a black mongrel fouling one corner of the grass. Then a boy entered the frame of Sam's view, riding a yellow BMX. He neatly jerked the front wheel in the air, and cycled slowly on the rear wheel along the further side of the grass, as if he had all the time in the world. As he reached the far corner, he suddenly dropped the front wheel and, leaning forward determinedly, peddled hard and raced out of Sam's sight . . . Down the hill? Down the hill to the High Street junction? Sam felt a sense of panic, like a bang in the ribs; he breathed heavily on the pane, steaming it up and clouding out the view below.

He stood quite still, hands by his sides, doing the slow, deep breathing his mother had taught him; felt the jerk of his heartbeat gradually subside, until it settled into a natural rhythm, like the hum of the central-heating system.

"Anyway, it looks brand new," he muttered. "I'll bet the brakes are sharp."

He walked into the kitchen and gathered his maths books and pencil case from the shelf, tossing them crossly on the table. He knew that his homework — decimals — was a mess; he had half an hour to correct it before Mrs Hooper arrived. Sitting at the table he stared moodily at his exercise book, the crossings-out and smudgy rubber marks, the doodles in the margin.

When the doorbell rang, exactly on the stroke of 9.30, his homework was unchanged, except for additional doodles and one more murky erasure.

Mrs Hooper, having neatly hung her coat, scarf and hat in the hall and placed her lumpy handbag by the breadboard — she always put it there — looked through his work in silence.

Why doesn't she ever lose her temper, wondered Sam. It's so maddening.

Mrs Hooper laid down her red biro and looked sad. "This isn't very good, Sam, is it? I think we'd better go through it again, don't you?"

Patiently she explained the decimal system, while Sam stared at the mole on the side of her neck. ". . . numbers *before* the point are whole . . . *after* the point are fractions . . . *must* line up the points . . . position of the zero is important . . ."

Zero. That's my life, thought Sam, and no point to it. He gritted his teeth, disgusted at his self pity. Pressing his fists into his cheeks, he willed himself to concentrate, and watched Mrs Hooper's freckled hand morse-coding down the maths book.

"Are you with me now, Sam? Right, we'll go through these questions again."

Sam picked up his biro. The quicker he got the point, the sooner she'd go.

"Hello, love." Mrs Leonard slung her coat and scarf over the back of a chair and bent to kiss the top of her son's dark head. "I'm sorry I'm late; I got held up. What are you working at?"

Sam lined his forearm across the exercise book, and started to draw a careful spiral in one corner of the page. A slight frown creased his mother's forehead. With an effort she smiled and smoothed out the frown lines with index and middle finger. "I've plonked a bag of shopping in the hall," she said. "Could you be a dear and unload it in the kitchen for me? I've had a beastly morning. I must just sit for a moment."

Sam closed his exercise book, pushed back his chair and slouched out of the small sitting-room.

His mother hovered indecisively by the table Sam sometimes used as a desk, then flipped open the exercise book until she located the spiral on the left-hand corner. She struggled to decipher Sam's careless scrawl.

She smiled, then guiltily closed the book. She remembered how angry she had been as a girl herself, when her mother had read a letter to a schoolfriend that she had left lying about. It was wrong to snoop on Sam — he had a right to his own privacy — but she worried so about him. With a sigh she turned from the table and followed him into the kitchen.

He was unloading the shopping on the kitchen table. Lightly she touched his shoulder, then took up the kettle and filled it at the sink. "Leave the ham, crisps and tomatoes on the table. We'll have them for lunch."

While they were eating, Mrs Leonard asked Sam about

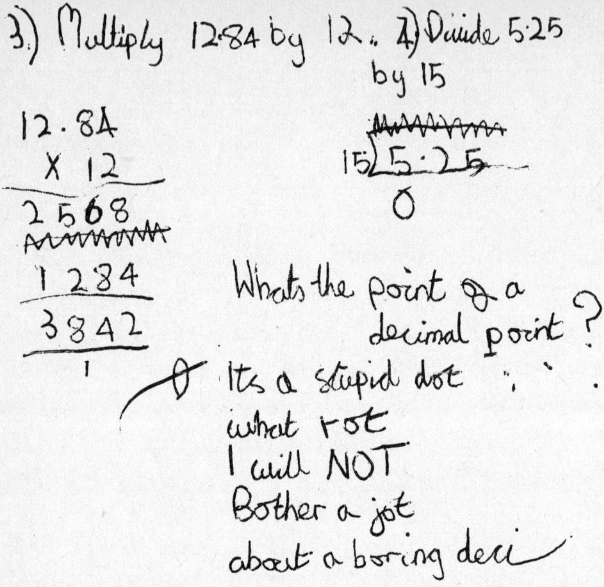

his morning. His response was monosyllabic. "What's Mrs Hooper given you for your homework?" she pressed him.

"Oh. Maths. And one or two other things."

"Try and get it over with after lunch. I'm afraid I've got a pile of typing to do. Then we'll go out somewhere."

"Okay, Mum."

While his mother banged away at her typewriter in her bedroom, Sam spread his maths books over the kitchen table and stared at them disconsolately. He found he hadn't a clue where to begin. He stabbed his pencil repeatedly at the page, scouring it with savage little lead pricks.

He didn't notice the silence in place of the familiar clackety-clack of his mum's portable typewriter, and started when her hands curved round his shoulders.

"Have you done it?"

He writhed his shoulders to throw off her hands. "Give me time, Mum."

"Sam, you haven't done anything. And what are these . . .?" She reached over him and picked up the decimated exercise book. Snatching it from her, Sam leapt to his feet. "Don't nag, Mum." He could hear his voice rising to a whine, and recognized the tension in his mother's hands, as her fingers spread and stiffened.

"Sam, you've got to buckle under. If you don't get on with your work under Mrs Hooper, you may have to go away to a special school — or something. You can't stay at home for ever. They'll insist you go back to school; it's the law. It's not good for you, cooped up in here. You must get out more. Make friends. You must —."

Sam snapped his book shut, wedging it under his arm. "Must! Must!" he yelled. "I don't want to be a boring mathematician. I don't need friends. What school? What *special* school? I'm never going to school again, never ever. You're horrible. To hell with Mrs Hooper!" He slammed the kitchen door and ran into his bedroom, diving into his bed — shoes and all — under the duvet.

In the dark warmth of his den his anger became muffled and absorbed. His thoughts reluctantly turned to his mother. She would be making a pot of tea; she always made one when she was upset and always, automatically, for two. She would sit very upright at the kitchen table and stir non-existent sugar round and round her cup. When she was upset she still forgot that she'd given up sugar.

She never complained about her job — typing for a firm of solicitors — though he knew she found the work tiring. Utterly boring, too. He had tried to read a will she had been typing at home, and he didn't understand one single word of it. When he asked her to explain, she had frowned, then smiled shyly and shrugged. She didn't understand it either. They had moved from London to Worple because of the job; it wasn't easy to get part-time work anywhere. At least they were together in the afternoons, and on Friday mornings, the day Mrs Hooper did not come, Sam was allowed to ring her at the office if he wanted.

Perhaps, he fretted, they should have gone to Australia. His mother had suggested it after Dad died. He mother and stepfather were in Sydney; Dad's parents and brother in a place called Dubbo. But the thought of going to a strange country, full of ex-convicts, had filled Sam with dread. He was terrified of snakes; and what about the heat — he hated being too hot. He didn't know their families; how can you call a stranger "Grandma"? So they had not gone. Was Worple any less foreign than Dubbo or Sydney?

I can look after her, he assured himself. She doesn't need anyone else. I'm her family.

Inside his feathered nest, from a distance, he heard a series of taps. He raised a corner of the duvet and cautiously peered out, blinking rapidly in the onslaught of light.

It was his mother knocking on his door. "Supper's ready. Spaghetti bolognese."

He let the duvet fall, and crouched under it, not answering; waiting for the door to open, for her competent hands to unwrap him. But this time she did not come.

He peeled back the duvet, just a little at a time, so that the light filtered in gradually, not teasing his eyes. Then slowly he uncurled from the foetal position, like a new-born creature tentatively testing out its limbs, until he sat up on the edge of the bed, with his legs dangling. He rose from the bed and scuffed his feet towards the door.

His mother was half-way through her own plateful when Sam appeared, with tousled hair, and silently fetched his plate from under the grill.

"I thought we'd have an early supper. Then we can go out for a walk," she said, too brightly.

"I don't want to go out," he replied sulkily. "Anyway," he glanced at her slyly, "I've got my homework to do."

Two

"It's a lovely bright day, Sam," said his mother on Saturday morning, as she cleared away the breakfast things. "Shall we go to the park? We could fly your kite."

"I don't feel like going out," Sam replied. "It'll be freezing up on the hill." And what was the point in flying a kite without his dad?

"Well, how about a walk into town? We could have a burger at Macdonalds, and then a film."

"Mum, I don't want to go anywhere. I'm okay here." Seeing his mother's concerned face he added hastily, "We can play Monopoly or something."

His mother chose not to argue. She didn't want a repeat of last Thursday night.

"I know," she said, trying to sound bright, "let's sit down and plan your birthday."

Sam stared at her. "My birthday," he repeated stupidly.

"Sam. Surely you haven't forgotten! It's your birthday next Wednesday. We could . . . well, couldn't we invite some children round and have a party?"

Sam folded his arms. "A party! A birthday party! Funny hats and silly games. Mother."

She winced. Perhaps eleven was too old for conventional birthday parties. "Not that kind of party. I meant just one or two friends. We could have a slap-up tea and —."

"Friends!" he jeered. "What friends?"

Fighting back a sudden desire to shake her son, Mrs Leonard hissed, "You really are an ungrateful brat sometimes! No friends! Whose fault do you think *that* is?"

Sam eyed her stonily. "Yours," he said.

Snatching up the duster, which hung over the radiator, Mrs Leonard rushed out of the kitchen.

"I hate parties. I hate birthdays. I don't need friends." Sam stood pale and taut by the kitchen table. "And I hate your rotten duster," he yelled.

His mother froze in the hall, the duster clutched in her hand.

"Oh God," she groaned, and began to dust the hall radiator.

Sam felt numb. He remembered the biblical story of Lot and the pillar of salt, and understood how Lot's wife must have felt. His mouth felt dry and crusty. Tentatively, he licked his lips; the taste was salty. If Lot's wife had licked hers, she would have eroded herself away. Could that pillar of salt hear and see? If God punished by turning her into an unfeeling block, then that wasn't so bad. But if she could see and hear and do nothing about it, that was some punishment.

Sam heard and saw far more than he let on. He knew that his mother cried a lot at night, that Mrs Hooper was concerned about him; he knew how tired his mum was, how much she missed Dad — and London.

If he had regularly checked his brakes, the way Dad had shown him; if he hadn't free-wheeled (always forbidden) down Headhill Street with the wind behind him to meet his dad at the junction. If, if, if — his father would be alive today. His eleventh birthday would be something to look foward to. Mum would be happy and he would be out in the sun today, flying his kite with Dad, or packing a picnic and a flask of tea to keep themselves warm while they queued for a Chelsea home match.

The silence in the cramped flat weighed on him. The only sound was the banging of blood in his temples. He felt that his head was about to burst. Mum was out there somewhere — a wall away, a world away — doing idiotic things with that horrid yellow duster. Blank and dry-eyed, he wished he could shrink to a knee-high toddler and bury his face in her knees. But his head reached above her shoulder and he was a boy — why, almost a man — and blubbering was out.

He shook his head violently, like a dog plagued by a wasp, and movement flowed back into his limbs. He settled himself at the kitchen table and forced his mind to his homework.

Sam woke with a sinking feeling. He had lain awake for hours the previous night, listening to his mother clattering about in the kitchen. He knew she was baking him a cake. He had heard the crisp crackle of paper as she wrapped his present, then the whoosh of water as she ran her bath. She hadn't got to bed till 2.00 a.m.

He would have to be cheerful; she had worked so hard. He was still lying in bed when she tapped at his door. He closed his eyes and turned his face to the wall. The door opened and he heard a faint clink as his mother set a mug of tea on his bedside table.

"Sam." Gently she shook him. "Time to get up, lie-abed. It's eight o'clock."

Sam yawned and stretched, feeling a fake.

"Morning, Mum," he mumbled.

She was still there standing by his bed.

Reluctantly, he sat up and rubbed his eyes.

"Happy birthday, sweetheart." She bent down and wrapped her arms around him, pressing her warm cheek against his. She smelled nice. He wished they could stay like this until the day was over.

"Come on," she said, giving him another shake. "I've got to go to work soon." She let him go. "Drink your tea while it's hot." She pulled the pillows from under his head, plumped them, and propped them up against the wall. Handing him the mug of tea, she perched on the edge of his bed.

"I didn't know whether to take a day off." She frowned, and looked at him with some concern. "But you did say —. Well, I thought perhaps you'd prefer to have a normal day."

"It's all right, Mum. I don't mind." He sipped the strong, hot tea. "Business as usual." He smiled at her, and she stretched out her hand and gave his a squeeze.

"Don't be long," she said.

Sam leaped out of bed and threw on his clothes with speed, not because he was excited at last at the prospect of his birthday, but in an attempt to engineer an enthusiasm he could not feel.

Stacked neatly beside his cereal bowl were two box-shaped parcels and an envelope. He was relieved to see that the wrapping paper was plain green; no silly pictures. He opened the envelope first. It, too, was tactfully undemonstrative; a picture of a clipper sailing-ship riding a choppy sea and, "Happy Birthday Sam. Love, Mum" inside. He glanced up gratefully at his mother, who was buttering her toast, and gave her a quick, shy smile.

He next opened the smaller of the two parcels. It was a book about World War II. "Thanks, Mum," he said.

"Aren't you going to open the other one?" His mother sounded slightly breathless.

Sam carefully unsealed the strips of sellotape and slipped the paper off. A neat leather case with a strap. He unclasped the case and drew out a pair of binoculars.

"Mum," he breathed. He ran out to the small sitting-room and opened the door leading on to the balcony. Raising the binoculars to his eyes he saw nothing but a blur. He experimented with the eyepiece hinge and the focussing ring. The blurry image began to sharpen, until he was looking at a large, redbrick house, so smothered with some kind of creeper that the windows looked like strange little burrows. A tall, unclipped hedge and a round-shaped tree with reddish leaves almost entirely hid the lower part of the house.

Slowly he panned the binoculars to the left, following the course of the hedge, until it came to a shaggy end at a low, broken-down gate. A narrow passage led from the gate and along the side of the house, where two dustbins stood like daleks.

Sam lowered his binoculars, and tried to identify the house, which had seemed to be just across the grassed court below. There were the two other tower blocks and the council houses on the estate, rows of houses curving down the hill, the primary school at the bottom. In the valley a jumble of office blocks, shops and houses. Up the other side more shops, a church tower, more office blocks, and tier upon tier of houses, like striated cliffs. He could not find the big house.

He peered through his binoculars again, veering them this way and that. A shop front with a red and white striped awning, a black cat on a wall, a man wobbling on a bicycle and scaffolding zoomed at him, so that he felt a little dizzy. A shaggy hedge sped past, a gate hanging off its hinges, an overgrown garden. Grasping the binoculars tight — for he felt that they were directing him, not he them — he held them still. A large redbrick house, but not the same, with a jungly garden at the side. He must have swivelled the glasses too far to the left. Slowly, taking care to hold the heavy glasses steady, he moved them to the right, and saw again the broken gate, the passageway and dustbins. The lids of the dustbins had been removed, and an old man was leaning over them.

He was scrabbling in one, throwing things out over his shoulder like a dog at a rabbit hole. Was he a tramp looking for food? Sam could scarcely believe that anyone in England could be *that* hungry. In his frantic hunt, his head sometimes vanished quite inside the dustbin. He was wearing a brown checked dressing-gown, and when his head at last re-emerged, Sam saw with delight that he had a sort of helmet on his head, multi-coloured.

The old man stood upright and turned, so that Sam saw his beaky nose and a narrow-lipped mouth clenched round a pipe. He tensed, expecting the man to yell at him, "Here. What do you think you're doing? Scarper!" But of course, the man could not possibly see him. He had been interrupted by a woman in a grey coat, with a dog on a lead, who was leaning in at the gateway. They spoke for a moment, then the old man replaced the lids and disappeared up the passage and round the back of the house. The woman continued on up the road with her dog. So he wasn't a tramp; he lived there.

He ran back into the kitchen. "Thanks, Mum. They're fantastic. You can see everything so clearly."

She beamed. She hadn't seen that bright look on her son's face in a long while. "Well," she said, pouring some muesli into his bowl, "you spend so much time looking out of the window, I thought they might be useful. You can tell me all about the goings-on in Worple when I get home at lunchtime."

She put her breakfast things in the sink and kissed him. "Have a lovely day."

Sam went back out on the balcony again, and through his binoculars studied that part of Worple which was visible between the tower blocks. He knew very little of the town beyond the area that comprised the council estate with its local shops; and Park Hill Road, dipping steeply down to the local primary school he had briefly attended, to the junction at the bottom which led to Worple High Street.

From his balcony, perched on the ninth floor of the tower block like an eagle's eyrie, he could just see the roof of Park Hill Primary, with its clock tower. It was funny how all schools looked the same; you knew at once they were schools.

Though he could not see them, he could hear the clamour of the children's voices in the playground. The strident dong, bong of the assembly bell sliced across their voices, so that he was suddenly aware of the steady sound of traffic further down the hill at the junction.

"At bong number one they all started to run, like a warren of rabbits upset by a gun." It was like William I's curfew, the school bell. Dong, bong! No more talking; in you go. If you want your mum or your dad, it's just too bad.

He had liked school before. Plenty to do; no time to be bored. And friends. He was good at making friends.

"It's all right, Mum," he had reassured her on his first day at Park Hill Primary. "It'll be a bit sticky at first, but I'll make new friends." He had ducked his head when she leant concernedly towards him by the school gate, and had lightly cuffed her arm.

His teacher was nice. She had smiley eyes and a soft voice. She talked to you as if you were an adult. There was a boy in his class — Jack someone-or-other — who had looked okay. He liked cricket, too. They'd talked about Botham and Gower at break; Jack had cricket lessons sometimes with a friend of his dad's.

But it hadn't been the same, somehow. When he was at school he worried about home. Had he remembered to lock up properly? One day he had been so sure that he'd left his bedroom window open that he'd run home during morning break to check. Such a fuss! He'd only been away about fifteen minutes. "But who could get in through your window, Sam?" his mother had asked, after the headmaster had called her in. "People can't fly."

He was concerned that his mother had too much to do, so he carefully cleared the breakfast table after she left for work, washed up, put away. But he got into trouble for being late. "It's all right, love. There's no need," his mother said. "I can do it when I get home at lunch. You mustn't be late." But there *was* a need. Someone must look after her.

He had begun to feel like a string puppet, with two puppeteers; one arm yanked this way, one that. When he looked after Mum, she worried about him not being at school; when he went to school, he couldn't concentrate because he was thinking about home. He had begun to feel sick in the mornings. He wasn't shamming, he really did feel sick. So she walked to school with him, and was probably late for work herself. Then they were both in trouble.

The church tower came into view. The clock said 9.25. Mrs Hooper would be here in a moment.

Special school? No fear; no special school, not any school for him. He hurried in and shut the glass balcony door. Taking up his English book, he checked yesterday's work. It must be right. If his work was good they would see that it was best to keep him at home. It must be ten out of ten.

Three

Mr Forbes opened the front door, lifted the bottle of milk from the doorstep, and with his free hand yanked at the paper which stuck through the letter flap. It would not budge. Cursing, he put the bottle down and tussled with the paper, which finally broke loose so suddenly that it sent him careering backwards down the hall. The damp cold had seeped through his night-clothes, scouring his meagre flesh. He banged the front door shut, and rubbed his hands against his thighs until he felt a painful rush of blood. He picked up the milk, the paper, and two buff envelopes which must have been jammed with the paper in the letter flap, and shuffled down the hall to the kitchen.

As he waited for the kettle to boil, he stared gloomily at the envelopes. Bills. Money had never seemed a problem when Ethel was alive, but now the lack of it rankled. Until eighteen months ago, and for many years before that, his elder sister Ethel had kept house for him. They had been born and grew up in this same house, the only surviving members of a family of six. Even in the last weeks of Ethel's life, when she was crippled with arthritis and recurring bronchitis, she had served up hot, homely meals and managed to keep their home warm and cosy. Now that she was gone, it was nothing but worry and discomfort.

Pushing the bills to one side, he made a pot of tea, then took up the paper and glanced at the front page. His attention was caught by a notice boxed on the top right-hand corner.

WIN £25,000 TODAY.
THE LUCKY NUMBER IS 106109

Mr Forbes choked on his tea.

After carefully reading the small print under the announcement, Mr Forbes removed the woollen tea cosy from the pot and pulled it over his head. It was comforting, not simply because it was warm and familiar but because Ethel had knitted it many years ago and he felt, somehow, that it might provide inspiration. He lit his pipe, wasting a great many matches, and then flapped in his down-at-heel slippers to the staircase, where he sat on the third-bottom stair to have a think. Where had he put all the recent newspapers? Ethel, he was sure, would have stacked them tidily somewhere, but he didn't think he had any such system. He got up, gripped his pipe firmly between his teeth, and began to hunt. He found some old *Daily Despatches*, too old, under the sideboard, a great stack, even older, in a cupboard in Ethel's bedroom, and the odd paper, or parts of one, scattered about in various corners providing, no doubt, nests for mice. Further search produced a few more *Daily Despatch* pages, yellow with age, used to line drawers; and one recent copy — but not the lucky one — stuffed down one of his Wellington boots, to dry it out; the heel had sprung a leak. In his wanderings from room to room of the big house, Mr Forbes lost sight of his objective and found himself leaning over the bath, prodding with his toothbrush end down the plughole. Muttering crossly at his absent-mindedness, he pressed his knuckles to his forehead.

"Twenty-five thousand pounds," he said out loud. "What could I do with — where could I —? Rubbish!" he exclaimed. "Rubbish collection isn't till Friday. Perhaps —."

He hurried down the stairs, unbolted the back door, and walked round the side of the house to where the two dustbins were kept. Throwing off the lids with a clatter, he began to rummage feverishly. He unearthed soggy *Daily Despatches* smeared with discarded baked beans, Smash, congealed tinned soup and blackened banana skins; shook out *Daily Despatches* filled with the blackened ash and used-up matches from his pipe trays; smoothed out a *Daily Despatch* still reeking of fish and chips. None of them bore the lucky number.

"Have you lost something?"

With a start, Mr Forbes looked up to meet the suspicious gaze of a smart woman in a grey coat, who was leaning in at the side gate.

"I — ah — I've found it," he said. Suddenly angry at being caught in such a humiliating activity (this was something tramps did) he barked, "Clear off. Mind your own business!" He gathered up the worst of the mess, wiped his hands on his dressing-gown, replaced the lids and, head well down to avoid those accusing eyes which he felt were still regarding him, he stomped back round the side of the house.

He climbed the stairs to the bathroom and ran a bath. His feet slipped while bending to stir the water and he barely saved himself from falling; there was something slimy on the sole of one slipper. His pyjamas were smeared with grime and some strands of congealed spaghetti were caught in one end of his dressing-gown cord. A glimpse of his ashen face in the mirror revealed a striped cheek and, worst of all, the tea cosy was still on his head in all its pink, mauve and yellow glory, tipped rakishly to one side.

"Oh, dear me," said Mr Forbes, sitting heavily on the bathroom stool. "Oh, dear." And then crossly, "I shall have a new fence. What right have they to pry?" He glowered at the bathroom window — which was partially screened by a page of newspaper that he had taped there recently to stop the draughts leaking through the crack in the pane. The page was upside down, and on the lower left-hand corner was a box containing a number.

"6-0-1-9-0-1" slowly read Mr Forbes. "No. That's not the

right number — but wait!" Carefully he untaped the page and turned it rightway up.

Mr Forbes took a deep breath, and a small pinprick of colour brightened his hollow cheeks. His knees felt a bit shaky. He was rich. No more worry about bills.

"I shall advertise for a quiet housekeeper who will mind her own business," he murmured, "and I shall open an account at Grove's Bookshop. Oh, the books I shall read."

Smiling contentedly, he turned off the taps.

After his bath, Mr Forbes phoned the *Daily Despatch* offices in London. He was put through to an efficient-sounding woman who told him to send the relevant corner of the front page of the lucky *Daily Despatch* to their office, "Attention Lucky Number Draw", enclosing his name, address and phone number.

"I think," said Mr Forbes, "I should prefer to deliver it myself."

The next day he took a train to London, and handed his *Daily Despatch* lucky number 106109 to the paper's head office. He caused quite a stir by refusing to give his address. "I know those reporters of yours. Sticking their noses where they're not wanted. I've rights, you know." It must be possible, he argued, to be given the cheque right now. If the draw was yesterday then the money must be around somewhere. "I don't want gangs of nasty reporters banging on my door," he said.

A number of telephone calls were made, and various *Daily Despatch* personnel — each looking rather more senior than the last — tried to persuade him to undergo a "little publicity". But the elderly man, in his threadbare coat and battered homburg hat, remained obdurate. He was sharp, too, for when a reporter slipped into the office and surreptitiously raised his camera to take a quick snap of the winner of the largest sweepstake the *Daily Despatch* had ever organized, the old man was too quick for him. The photographs, when developed, showed a lean frame in an overlarge coat, hat pulled well down over the face; it could just as well have been a coat rack.

After a couple of hours of hard bargaining, Mr Forbes received his cheque, and took the 2.40 from King's Cross, reaching home in time for tea.

While eating tinned spaghetti on toast, he composed the following advertisement, to be inserted in the *Worple Gazette*: *Wanted*: Mature housekeeper for retired gentleman. Salary negotiable. Must be discreet and reliable. Apply 27 Hillside, Worple.

Four

Sam made full use of the binoculars in the days following his birthday. Sometimes he allowed his mother to have a look, and showed her the redbrick houses on the hill. Once, he called her out on the balcony before breakfast to take a look at "the funny old man with the hat".

With the help of Mrs Hooper, who was delighted to see such rare enthusiasm in her moody pupil, he drew a careful plan of that section of Worple across the valley that he could scan through his binoculars. Using a street plan that his mother bought for him, he neatly wrote in all the street names and labelled the public buildings. He made detailed drawings of the seven large houses at the top of the hill, noting with delight that each was quite individual, one having dormer windows, another two oddly shaped chimney stacks, a third handsome pillars on either side of the smart front door.

As the row of seven houses was set a little apart, scooped into the steepest slope of the hillside, he was able to see their occupants entering and leaving their homes or working in their gardens. Houses further down the hill were jostled together, so that one street obscured details of the one above, and so Sam increasingly concentrated his binocular observations on this little community. He learned to predict their comings and goings, worked out likely relationships, gave them names. But it was the two houses on the westernmost side which most interested him.

The thin old man with the funny helmet, whom Sam had first picked out on the morning of his birthday, was his particular favourite. He lived in the sixth house in the row. He apparently lived alone and, apart from the milkman's deliveries, and a very occasional visit from the postman — for Sam's viewing sessions developed a sort of pattern on weekdays, a session before breakfast, another in the early afternoon, and a last check-up while his mother was preparing supper — he received no callers. He left the large, rambling house at 9.15 every weekday morning, and returned, generally, at about 2.00 p.m. The old man's solitariness appealed to Sam, and the fact that he always had a book under one arm. Mr Reader, he christened him, and decided that he was an eccentric miser who owned a second-hand bookshop.

The last house in the row, with a garden as overgrown and untended as Mr Reader's, but more easily visible because there was no high hedge at the front and the garden ran along the side of the house, was a mystery. It was clearly inhabited. The milkman and postman called regularly, and a van drew up outside every Thursday, the delivery man taking the goods round to the side entrance. As far as Sam could judge, they were mostly groceries. But apart from these men, Sam saw no one go in or come out.

It was on Tuesday, 9th April, that Sam first caught sight of an inhabitant of "No. 7". He remembered the date, because it was the same day that the Education Welfare Officer called. He was dreading Mrs Ellington's visit. His mother had reminded him of it the evening before, and he was accordingly uncommunicative at breakfast.

"You will agree to see her, Sam?" pleaded his mother. "She's very nice and she has your best interests at heart. She just wants to see how you are."

On her previous visit several weeks before, Sam had refused to say a word, and — when the snoopy woman had turned to his mum and asked her how she was coping with things at home, and her job — he had stormed out of the sitting-room and barricaded himself in his bedroom until long after she had gone.

"When's she coming?"

"Six o'clock. You will see her?"

"Yes. Okay, Mum, I'll be a good boy."

Feeling nervous and restless, Sam darted to his room as soon as the front door clicked behind his mother, picked up his binoculars, and went out on to the chilly balcony. He knew he ought to check over his work for Mrs Hooper — graphs and map reading — but his dread of the evening made concentration hopeless. He focussed immediately on the two now familiar end houses, numbers 7 and 6, but, realizing that No. 6 would give no satisfaction as Mr Reader would have gone off to his bookshop by now, he swivelled his glasses to the left and watched a ginger cat slinking between the bushes which grew raggedly near the side door of No. 7. All at once a girl emerged, a slender, pale creature with straight, fair hair which hung down to her shoulders. She bent down to stroke the cat, and then turned and looked back towards the side door as if in response to some other, unseen, person. Straightening up, she raised her head and seemed to stare across the valley straight at Sam; then turned, and went back indoors. He was so absorbed that he imagined he heard the click of the door as it shut. Who was she? Shouldn't she be at school? And who was the other, invisible, person? He was still leaning on the balcony with the binoculars glued to his eyes, when Mrs Hooper startled him.

"Goodness, Sam, you'll catch your death," she cautioned.

Reluctantly he lowered the glasses, and came in, shutting the door behind him.

"This winter will never end," said Mrs Hooper, looking sharply at Sam's purple hands. "I always find it impossible to concentrate when I'm too cold. Come on, we'll start with some exercises." She pushed the armchair to one side to clear a space.

"Right. Come and stand by me, dear." Clearly meaning business, she pushed her cardigan sleeves up to her elbows, and stretched bare, freckled arms out at shoulder level.

"Ah — one, two, up, down," she intoned, scissoring her arms and legs. Her short, reddish hair flopped wildly, and her left heel popped free of her flat slip-on, revealing a large hole in her stocking.

Panting slightly, Mrs Hooper gave a girlish laugh. "Come on, Sam. There's nothing like a bit of P.E. to get the circulation going and the brain whirring." Her smile faded as her pupil eyed her stonily. His shoulders were hunched, and two uncompromising lumps in the sides of his trousers indicated clenched fists buried in his pockets.

Mrs Hooper patted her hair and smoothed her skirt. "Very well, Sam," she said, still a little breathless. "I can see you're no sports enthusiast. Let's have a look at your graphs, shall we?"

Sam slouched to his table and drew out his chair with one foot.

To the accompaniment of Mrs Hooper's light voice and freckled hand, Sam wondered about the fair-haired girl on the hill. Perhaps she, too, was receiving home tuition because of some dark secret in her past. And who lived with her? Her mother? A widowed and gloomy father?

When Mrs Hooper rapped his hand and accused him of not concentrating, Sam felt venomous.

He snatched his maths exercise book from her, stabbed his finger at one of the graphs he had drawn the day before, and explained it to her — as if she were a slow pupil and he the teacher.

"*I* understand graphs, Sam," she said mildly. "And I'm pleased that you do, too." She paused a moment. "Now.

Perhaps you could show me the map you drew yesterday, and explain that to me, too."

Sam stared fixedly at his knuckles and made no move to open his geography book.

"Sam?"

"I'm good at maps," he said at last. "I don't need to explain it. I understand it."

"What's the matter, Sam?" asked Mrs Hooper gently. "Is it Mrs Ellington? Are you worried about her visit this evening?"

"No." Sam wanted to kick her. What business was it of hers? "Mrs Ellington's okay. I'm not worried about *her*."

"Good." Mrs Hooper's soft voice sounded faintly grainy. "Then there's absolutely no reason why we shouldn't do the map reading. Explain your map to me, Sam."

When Mrs Hooper left a little after 12.30, remarking "I'm sure Mrs Ellington will see a great improvement in you, Sam," he prowled restlessly about the small sitting-room. His brief freedom from the trauma of facing other people seemed threatened. "Why can't they leave me alone?" he cried.

Without bothering to touch the plate of salad his mother had left in the fridge for him as she was going to be home later than usual, he grabbed his binoculars and went out on the balcony again. The day had warmed up considerably, and the houses on the hill were bathed in a bright, clear light which defined each brick and slate. No people were visible, and the ginger cat had vanished. Sam amused himself by slowly training his binoculars on one window after another of No. 7, starting with the ground floor and working upwards, inventing a ground plan of the invisible interior. He thought he caught a glimpse, at the big first-floor window with the little balcony, of a movement behind the glass, but could not be sure. Tired of working with such inadequate material, he was about to lower the binoculars, when he saw the girl emerge from the side door.

Quickly, he pressed them to his eyes. There she was, standing in front of the bushes with her hands clasped in front of her. She turned her head towards the door, and then vanished inside again, reappearing a few moments later with a large basket of laundry. She staggered across the long grass and carefully lowered the basket to the ground underneath a tall tree near the side fence. Then she hurried indoors, emerging a little later with a coil of rope. That, too, was dropped by the basket. She then walked slowly and pensively to and fro beside the fence, glancing up at the trees and then, all at once decisive, ran back to the first tree and attempted to gain a foothold on the broad, smooth trunk. Several attempts proved useless. I bet I could manage that, Sam thought. She's wearing the wrong sort of shoes. She went back in, and reappeared some considerable time later with a large step-ladder, teetering slightly under its awkward weight. She set it up under the trees, tested it for firmness, and, taking one end of the rope in her left hand, carefully ascended the ladder until Sam could only see her white socks and strap shoes. Eventually a sagging clothes line was strung up alongside the fence, and the girl pegged up the washing, straining on tiptoe at either end, where she could barely reach. She folded the ladder and staggered indoors with it, collected up the empty basket, and then finally disappeared.

Sam studied the flapping clothes on the line, trying to find out more about the occupants of No. 7. Apart from sheets and pillow-cases there were apparently only female garments, including several strange sorts of bloomers. No man in the house, then. He remained on the balcony for some time in the hopes of seeing more of the girl, but the garden stayed empty, except for the drying clothes, which filled out and danced as if taunting him with their near-human gymnastics.

He trailed to the kitchen and worked his way through the salad without appetite. Having rinsed his plate and cutlery under the tap, he prowled about the flat, unable to fix his mind to anything. He felt raw and exposed.

Suddenly decisive, he went out to the hall and dialled his mother's office number.

"Good morning. Brown and Hoare."

"Could I speak to Mum — Mrs Leonard, please."

"Oh, hello. Just a moment, dear."

He held the earpiece at a distance as the familiar, sharp clicks told him the lady at the other end was transferring the call to his mother.

"Hello. Sam?"

"Hello, Mum."

"Everything all right, pet?"

"Yes." He paused, toying with the springy flex. "I saw a girl. She's pretty."

"A girl?"

"Mmm."

"Where? What girl? Did you talk to her?"

"No."

"Are you sure you're all right, love? Has Mrs Hooper gone?"

"Yes. I'm all right. I didn't talk to her. I just saw her — with the binoculars."

"Oh. I see." No. She didn't see at all. "I'm just finishing this, and then I'll come straight home, Sam. You're not worried, are you, about Mrs Ellington?"

Sam felt annoyed. Her, too.

"No. I'm okay. See you later."

"Goodbye, love, I'll be home soon."

He didn't dislike Mrs Hooper — he supposed she'd been pretty decent to him really — but he resented her knowing about his dad, about Mrs Ellington. That she should have guessed he was worried about Mrs Ellington's intended visit this evening seemed like an insult. He felt that both Mrs Hooper and Mrs Ellington were conspiring against him. He must form a plan of campaign.

Pacing thoughtfully between sitting-room, kitchen and hall, he drew up a mental list of the important points. As they began to take shape, he decided to approach them in a logical way; that's something his dad had taught him. He tore a page from the back of one of his personal notebooks, ruled a line down the centre, and headed the two halves "THEM" and "US".

Them	Us
1. Want us to go back to 'school	Not yet.
2. If not, a 'special school'	Definitly not
3. Improve school work	OK. Work harder
4. Want us to make friends	Don't need them.
5. Watching us like hawks.	Be secret as badger

Frowning at the list he had drawn up, Sam doodled his biro across the bottom of the sheet of paper. Wiggles and squirls, zigzags and dots. Then the letter "J", carefully blocked in with neat, oblique lines, followed by "E", "S", another "S", an "I", a "C" and an "A" with a decorated tail.

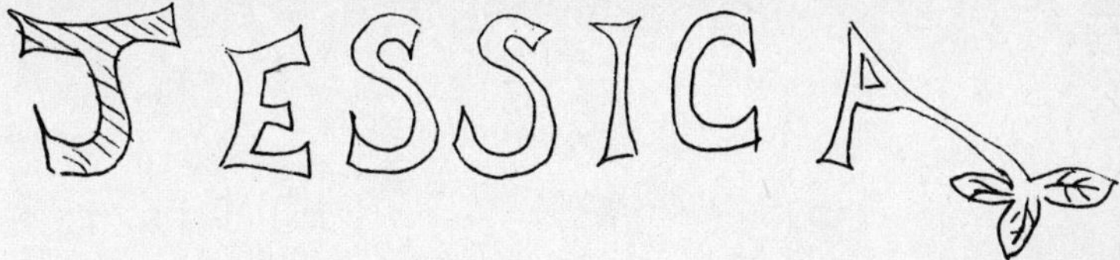

Sam needed an ally. The girl on the hill, isolated as he was, struggling to erect a washing line while other girls of her age were at school or playing with friends, seemed the natural person. "JESSICA". He and Jessica would beat the system somehow.

Five

By the time his mother returned, Sam had planned his campaign. He must be seen to be making progress, to keep everyone happy, but not so much progress that they would consider him ready for school.

He suspected that decisions as to his future were not simply dependent upon what he and his mother — or even perhaps Mrs Hooper — felt would be best. But if he could wangle things so that his mum, Mrs Hooper and Mrs Ellington all agreed, he might be able to win a breathing space.

Sam and his mother had a high tea, and he helped to plump up the cushions and get the flat clean and tidy for Mrs Ellington's visit. His mother's vigorous handling of the duster — he noticed that she polished the coffee table twice — told him that she was as nervous as himself.

Mrs Ellington, a short, sturdy woman with a brisk manner, arrived punctually. She accepted the offer of a cup of tea. While Mrs Leonard was making it, having declined Sam's offer to do so himself, Mrs Ellington asked him whether she could see some of the work he had been doing for Mrs Hooper.

He collected his exercise books and spread them out on the table for her. She showed a real interest, particularly in the work about Worple which had been inspired by the present of the binoculars.

"Did you do all this with Mrs Hooper?" she asked. "I gather you're very keen on writing. Have you any work of your own?"

Taken momentarily off guard, Sam nearly confided that he

had been writing about Mr Reader, the old man on the hill, but his mother's entrance with the tea stopped him. It had been a near thing.

"No," Sam replied. "Mrs Hooper gives me a lot of homework." Mrs Ellington smiled and his mother looked pleased.

"I had a word with Mrs Hooper the other day, Sam," said Mrs Ellington, "and she says you're beginning to work more steadily. You know, I think it's time you thought in terms of going back to school. What do you say?"

Mrs Leonard looked anxiously at her son, but he had adopted that withdrawn look that gave nothing away.

"Well . . ." He drew out the word in a slow breath. "I still find . . . I don't think. . . ." He floundered. "I haven't any friends," he ended lamely.

"But that's just it, Sam," said Mrs Ellington. "Of course you have no friends, confined to this little flat all day. School will bring you friends, and interests — all sorts of exciting new things. Education isn't just learning from books. You know that."

"Yes, but — I need more time." He picked up his pencil and began to roll it between his fingers. He knew they were both watching him and dared not look up. "I still find it hard to meet people . . ." He glanced surreptitiously at his mother.

She leant a little forward, smiling nervously. "Perhaps he shouldn't be rushed back to school," she said. "He's making such progress now. The last two weeks Mrs Hooper's been really pleased with him. He's more helpful round the flat — coming out of himself a bit. It would be terrible if we sent him back too early and undid all the good."

Mrs Ellington frowned. She looked far from convinced. "Sam is an intelligent and capable boy. This home tuition is a temporary measure, to give you both time to sort things out. It's not healthy for an 11-year-old boy to be so much on his own. Do you go out much, Sam?"

"Well, he went to the High Street with me last Saturday and —." Mrs Leonard sounded over-eager.

Mrs Ellington looked hard at Sam, not at his mother.

Sam felt angry. All this talking about himself as if he wasn't there. And now it seemed as if, in some indefinable way, his mother was under attack. This was clearly a case of Us and Them.

"I used to refuse to go out," he said, "but I went shopping with my mother last Saturday, as she said. And we walked in the park after."

Sam remembered only too well why he had agreed to go out with his mother that day. After breakfast she had suggested that they climb the opposite hill to take a closer look at the row of houses that Sam had been studying through his binoculars. He had been appalled at the thought. What if he came face to face with the old man, Mr Reader? It wouldn't be at all the same as seeing him framed in a circle of magnification. Would he just walk by as if they were strangers? But how could he, when he already knew Mr Reader so well? Hastily he had opted for shopping, followed by a brisk walk in the park above the council estate. He had been so determined to divert his mother from any return to the original suggestion that he had not worried about the strangers they encountered in the shops and park. He had talked non-stop, and had returned to their flat for tea with a healthy appetite and no sense of having been stared at and discussed.

He shook himself back to the uncomfortable present to find they were both still watching him carefully, as if he were a weird specimen in a jar. He was hit by a nauseating sense of isolation. It wasn't Them and Us. It was Them and Me. His mum was on Their side.

"They stare at me," he cried. "I can't bear them staring. Children are the worst." He clasped his arms tightly to his chest. Glaring at Mrs Ellington accusingly, he refused to turn and meet his mother's eye. Them and Me.

"You don't understand," he muttered through clenched teeth. "You're stupid and you don't understand." He wanted to shatter the silence. Punish them for taking his life in their hands. He picked up his china mug — half full of tea — and hurled it against the wall. It ricocheted off the wall and bounced onto the carpet, intact. A brown stain spread in spidery fingers down the wallpaper.

Suddenly feeling limp, he fell back into his chair and pressed his face into the arm, biting back tears.

"Oh, Sam." His mother's voice held a catch in it and Sam knew she wanted to put her arms around him. Well, just let her try!

"Sam." Mrs Ellington sounded calm, and Sam was grateful for that. "I think your mother and I should have a talk. Would you like to be on your own for a bit?"

With his face still buried in the velvety fabric of the armchair, he vigorously nodded his head. "Shall we go into the kitchen, Mrs Leonard?"

He did not move after they had left, quietly closing the door behind them. Had he planned the whole thing? He didn't know. Would this help him, give him the extension he wanted, or had he wrecked his chances? He didn't know that, either.

He heard the faint murmur of their voices through the wall, but he had no desire to eavesdrop. They were planning his future, discussing him, peeling the layers off him like an onion. Well, he hoped it made their eyes water.

"He hasn't been like this — not in the past few weeks." Sophie Leonard's defiant defence of Sam sounded feeble. "He's been so much better. Really he has."

"Let us sit down," said Mrs Ellington, not unkindly. She drew out two kitchen chairs. "The fact is, this isolation can't be doing Sam much good. It leads to too much introspection. He's missed nearly a term and a half of school already."

"I know. Believe me, Mrs Ellington, I worry about him a lot. But — he's started to come out of his shell. He's beginning to show an interest in things."

"That's good. Encourage that as much as you can." She looked thoughtful. Opening the folder that she had brought with her into the kitchen, she flipped through it. "What about the nightmares? Have these continued?"

"No. He's sleeping well."

"Does he speak of his father at all? Of the accident?"

"No." Mrs Leonard winced. "Not really. The fact is we both find it so painful."

"Of course." Mrs Ellington smiled sympathetically. "Talking can help," she said. "You as well as him. I wonder whether" — she paused — "a few sessions of child guidance might not be helpful."

"Oh no!" Mrs Leonard involuntarily pressed her fingers to her mouth. "Not that."

"But Mrs Leonard —"

"I know. It's silly of me to react like this. I don't know much about such things; perhaps it would help. But I do know Sam, Mrs Ellington. I *do* know my son. I don't think —." She took a deep breath, and started again. "I'm not putting this very well, but I think Sam is his own best medicine. I think he's working things out. I feel that he's grappling with something, and that he is getting somewhere. He's very independent, you know, like his father. He likes Mrs Hooper — and you — but he resents your interference, too. Bringing someone else in . . . Mrs Ellington, I believe that would make him very angry. It could push him straight back into the shell which he has recently begun to peep out of."

"So what do you suggest?"

"Leave things as they are. Give him more time. If he goes to

Park Hill Primary — or wherever — it would only be for one term. Mightn't that be awfully disruptive?"

Mrs Ellington looked hard at Sam's mother. "Very well," she said at last. "I'll see what we can do. I can't promise anything, mind."

"Thank you, Mrs Ellington."

After Mrs Ellington left, Sam's mother hurried into the sitting-room. He was curled up in the same chair, in much the same position as they had left him, except that his right arm now hung limply across the chair arm. He was fast asleep. She was relieved that she would not have to palm him off with half-assurances tonight; there would be no point in raising his hopes while nothing was yet settled.

She scooped him up and half-carried, half-dragged him to his bedroom. What a weight her boy was. He mumbled once or twice, and sluggishly moved one limb, then another, to help her in the awkward task of getting him undressed and into his pyjamas.

"You old baby," she said affectionately, as she peeled off the second sock. "Sleep now." She snuggled the duvet around him and kissed his forehead.

He is flying in a tunnel of wind. The pedals spin, dissolving into a circle. He gulps cold air; it seems a solid thing, too thick to breathe. Walls, doors, bollards sweep past on either side. Tensing fingers and thumb, he grips the brake — presses harder and harder, till hands, arms, teeth even, seem made of steel. But still he flies on, towards giant red letters on a yellow background.

ROOTS

The letters start to throb, to spin about, dissolve into a blur. Then, coalescing in a different configuration, he reads

Two staring "O"s, a volatile "R" that gapes and writhes and cries: "Stop, Sam. Stop!" The silence is torn apart with screech of tyres, the clink of breaking glass. One human cry. Then emptiness.

Mrs Leonard heard the scream above the flat newsreader's voice. "Daddy! Daddy, stop!"

She ran into Sam's room and, catching her heels in the duvet which was bundled on the floor by his bed, she stumbled to him.

"It's all right, love, it's all right. Shhh, Sam." Gently she soothed the taut, struggling body.

"He's dead. He's dead," keened Sam, rocking. "I broke his face."

"It was a dream."

"No. I killed him. I broke his face."

Together they rocked, physically bound yet isolated each in their own misery.

When at last they were calmer, Sam's mother made two cups of cocoa, which they sipped together on his bed.

"Was it a nightmare about Daddy?" she probed.

Sam nodded.

"It's the first time in weeks," she said, more to herself than to him. Then, looking keenly at Sam, "What brought it on? Was it Mrs Ellington's visit?"

Suddenly Sam felt wide awake. He stared into his mug of cocoa. He was frightened. He had started to tell people things — he had even nearly told Mrs Ellington, of all people, about his secret world. And where had it got him? He was threatened by school, and now, once again, by nightmares. He must be careful. He felt the warmth of his mother's body beside him; not quite touching him but as real and lovely as a cat's purr. Why did schools and Mrs Ellington have to barge in; they had been doing all right, the two of them.

"I know I've got to go to school," he said carefully. "But not so soon. Can't I stay at home until I go to secondary school?"

His mother hesitated; then, putting her mug on the bedside table, she placed her hands over his warm ones, as they cradled his hot mug.

"I've already suggested that to Mrs Ellington. She's going to discuss it with a few people. I agree you need more time." She smoothed back his hair, and pressed her forehead against his, so that he could see himself reflected in her iris. "You must tell me when things worry you, pet. Talking helps. I know it's not easy, with me working and everything, but I think we should both try."

Sam gave a little nod. He didn't trust himself to speak, for he was not a good liar. He only knew that, whatever happened, he was going to keep himself at a distance from the adults in his life.

"Do you think you'll sleep now?"

He nodded again and passed his mug to her. She picked up

the duvet, shook it out and tucked it round him. "Would you like me to stay with you for a bit?"

"Yes."

She curled up beside him and gently stroked his hair, then his eyelids so he had to close them, then his hair again. She began to sing softly. He loved her singing voice; it was not at all like her speaking one, but sort of husky and blurry.

"My darling, why I sing this song
  Is easy to explain.
It tells what happens all along
  The bridges of the Seine.
The vagabonds go there at night
  To sleep all their troubles away . . ."

He felt deliciously floaty. When her hand lay still in his hair, he stirred his head drowsily to urge it into movement.

At last she rose quietly from his bed. He felt too sluggish to complain.

"Goodnight, pet," she whispered. "Call me if you need me."

Six

Within a week of placing his advertisement for a housekeeper in the *Worple Gazette*, Mr Forbes received two applications. He wrote short replies to both, asking them to come for an interview at 27 Hillside, on Saturday 30th March, at eleven and eleven thirty respectively.

"Either they'll be right, or they won't," he reasoned. "A few minutes will tell."

Since Ethel's death, Mr Forbes had taken to spending most weekday mornings in the central Worple library. It was warm in there; he could read to his heart's content, and no one bothered him. If he felt sociable, which was rarely, the librarians were quite friendly, and there was always someone browsing through the daily papers with whom he could exchange comments about the state of the world.

This morning, however, the prospect of someone to keep house for him made him feel adventurous. He left home at his usual time, but walked down Church Street to Grove's Bookshop instead of taking his usual route to the library. He browsed along the bookshelves and, after much consideration, selected three large hardbacks — a biography, a new thriller and a historical novel. He calculated that the three books would cost him £31.85.

"Phew," he whistled under his breath. "That's a bit excessive." He juggled indecisively with the three books, wondering which to replace. But that spirit of adventure still tingled in him.

Bracing his narrow shoulders in their ill-fitting coat, he

advanced on the cash counter. "I'll take all these," he said boldly, "and" — his eyes sparked — "I'd like to see the manager."

"Seeing managers" was a new experience for him and he found he rather enjoyed it. He told the manager that he wished to open a regular account at the bookshop, and that he would like a monthly list of all new books coming into the shop, "especially detective stories and adventure stories. I like those — or history."

The waxy-faced manager studied the scruffy old man doubtfully. "Well, I don't know, sir. This is rather unusual."

"I shall make it worth your while," said Mr Forbes. "As from next month, I shall send you a regular order for any books that I require, and I'll settle the bill every quarter. I should like the books to be delivered to my home. I shall be too busy to collect them myself."

"Are you a bibliophile?" asked the manager curiously.

"That's impertinent," Mr Forbes retorted. He decided to buy a good dictionary while he was in Grove's.

On Saturday morning Mr Forbes struggled with the heavy Hoover. He hated housework, and disliked the Hoover's hungry roar. The flex got twisted around the legs of the table on the upstairs landing and he crossly switched it off. The front door knocker was rattling.

"You're late," he growled, as he opened the door to a small, thin woman with a worried expression.

"I tried —" faintly explained the harassed woman.

"You'd better come in," interrupted Mr Forbes. She hadn't the confidence to explain that she had been rapping at the door and vainly pressing the doorbell, which clearly didn't work, for some minutes.

"Someone else is coming in fifteen minutes," grumbled Mr Forbes. "*If* she's punctual — so we'll have to be quick."

He shuffled to a stop halfway along the ill-lit hall, and turned to face her.

"Can you cook plain food?" he asked. "Have you many friends?" He glanced sharply at her hands, which were clasped around her handbag, against her stomach. "Are you married or single?"

Quite at a loss, the nervous woman plucked at her coat sleeve. "I never married, Mr . . .. It was Mother, you see," she began timidly. "I kept house for her." He had turned again, and continued down the hall to a door at the end. "I have a few friends. There's Molly, and Suzy, and Mrs Simms," she whispered, following him, "and young Billy who helps with odd jobs — a nice boy, Billy. But the house is too big now Mother's passed away, and I thought, when I saw the advertisement . . ."

Her faint treble trailed away, and she stopped irresolutely just inside the door of a small, stuffy sitting-room.

"You won't be suitable," said the strange man, looking at her fiercely. "No friends. I can't be having friends, and noisy boys, bothering me."

"But I won't bring —" pleaded the woman, as she was conducted back down the hall to the front door.

"Good day," he said, bundling her on to the porch, and he firmly shut the door.

He had just reached the top of the stairs, intending to stow away the Hoover, when he heard the door-knocker again. Two smart raps, then silence. He glanced at his watch. It was exactly eleven thirty.

He opened the door to a large woman, half a head taller than himself, whose eyes, sharp and bright, met his own squarely.

"Mrs Butts, sir," she said. "Come for the post of housekeeper."

He led her along the hall to the sitting-room, and indicated a chair.

"I'll stand, if it's all the same," she said.

Mr Forbes, who was in the act of lowering his lean behind into his favourite armchair, was disconcerted. Catching hold of the chair arms, he levered himself to a standing position. The remainder of the interview was conducted upright.

He cleared his throat and eyed her slyly from under beetle brows. "What meals can you cook?"

"Plain home cooking. I don't go in for fancy things myself."

"Married?"

"No."

"Friends?"

"One or two. But I don't see as that's revelant. I'll not bother *you* with them."

"And you would be content to live in?"

"I'll have to, sir, seeing as I don't have a place of my own."

"I'll need references," said Mr Forbes.

Silently, she opened her capacious handbag and dug out a white envelope, which she handed to him. "They was my previous employers," she explained.

He unsealed the envelope and read the letter, from a Mrs Flynn; it was plainly worded, and praised Mrs Butts' good sense, honesty, efficiency and excellent cooking.

"I see you worked for the Flynns for fifteen years. Why are you leaving them now?"

"Mr Flynn died last year, sir. His wife has decided to move into a little flat near her daughter. There's no place there for me."

"You'll do," said Mr Forbes. "When can you start?"

They discussed money; Mr Forbes was impressed by Mrs Butts' business acumen. She had a clear idea of what she was worth and what she would need in the way of expenses. She indicated that she would be content to organize the housekeeping and garden maintenance, and her estimates of what these would cost seemed remarkably accurate.

It was settled that she should move in on the fourteenth of April, a Sunday. She would have the big back bedroom, baths in the evening, and the front sitting-room, with the large-screen television that Ethel had treasured, for her own use. She could do as she liked in the afternoons, and have Mondays and the last weekend of the month off. No visitors on the premises, and he didn't want chatter and nosy questions.

"I know how to keep myself to myself," said Mrs Butts.

Mrs Butts moved in on the Sunday with the minimum of fuss. Not one to waste time, she bustled silently about the large house raising clouds of dust as she rubbed and scoured and polished. Before the week was out, the windows were bright, the once uniformly grey carpets bloomed with splashes of red, blue and gold, and faded antique wood exuded a scent of good old-fashioned furniture polish. Bright daffodils on a side table brought a touch of cheer to the gloomy hall, and pots and pans gleamed from their hooks on the kitchen wall. Mr Forbes made no comment, though he inwardly applauded her industry.

Mrs Butts had found an immense accumulation of junk about the house, which she deposited in the disused back bedroom. She mentioned this to Mr Forbes one evening, as she served him his shepherd's pie.

"No books," said Mr Forbes shortly, looking up from his thriller. "They must be left exactly where they are. Do what you like with the rest."

Mrs Butts pursed her lips and neatly ladled more peas onto his plate. "Very good, sir."

She was taking a sip of water between mouthfuls when her employer startled her by barking. "Tea cosy!"

She put down her glass. "Tea cosy?"

"Tea cosy must not be categorized as junk."

"Well," gasped Mrs Butts, who was not easily surprised. "So you'd want me to keep that tea cosy."

"I would."

The rest of the meal passed in silence.

As soon as Mr Forbes had retired to his sitting room, Mrs Butts climbed the stairs to the back bedroom and rummaged through the pile of rubbish.

"Tea cosy!" she snorted. "What would the man be wanting with that nasty thing?" Once found, she replaced it in the kitchen drawer where she had first discovered it.

She arranged for a young man she knew to collect the junk and dispose of it. She also persuaded him — for a small fee — to tidy up the overgrown front garden.

Seven

Cautiously, Sam set out to prove that he was all right. He was attentive in Mrs Hooper's lessons, steering her always on the safe tack of a fixed curriculum, so that she soon stopped asking him what he had been doing in his own time, satisfied with the quality of the work that she had initiated. With his mother he was distantly courteous, using his work as a screen to ward off more personal enquiries. He became more helpful round the flat, and volunteered to buy small groceries from the arcade of local shops on the estate.

He went along with — even encouraged — occasional weekend outings, to the park, the cinema, the High Street and, as the weather improved and the hillsides were bright with primroses and daffodils, trips to the countryside and outlying villages. These outings served a dual purpose. They gave him an outlet for his burgeoning energies, and created a sense of closeness and things shared with his mother.

Mrs Leonard became more relaxed, her smiles less rare. Her son was growing sturdier and, though she regretted the passing of a scruffy, dynamic little boy, she felt a shy pride in the emergence of this serious, enquiring companion.

She had insisted upon an interview with Mrs Ellington, Mrs Hooper and the educational psychologist. They had finally agreed that a single term at the school might not be beneficial to Sam. So long as his work continued to improve, it might be best to continue with the present arrangement until he went up to secondary school in September.

Her attempts to introduce other children of his age to their home had so far met with no success, but occasionally on their outings he had exchanged smiles, even interested comments, with children they had encountered, and she felt sure that it would only be a matter of time before he actively sought friends.

His private notebooks, which had once been left carelessly around the flat, Sam now stowed away in the shelf on top of his wardrobe. He took them down only when he had the flat to himself. He continued to use the binoculars, methodically sifting the information they supplied into two categories: public and private. Mrs Hooper and his mum admired his accurate drawings of houses, the church tower and office blocks, and were impressed, even a little awed, when he brought home books from the library and regaled them with information about different styles of roof, various methods of laying bricks, the advantage of using concrete in a mysterious process called "battery casting".

"It sounds like a terrible Alice in Wonderland game," remarked his mother. "Whacking poor little hens about."

His sketches of Jessica, Mr Reader, and the large lady in black who had mysteriously moved in with the old man, they did not see. Nor the journal in which he wrote about them.

At first Sam thought the "dark lady" was just visiting Mr Reader. This was odd enough, since he never had visitors. But when, twice in one week, Sam saw her dark-coated bulk, a shopping bag over one arm, march out through the gap in the hedge a little after 9.00 a.m., he became puzzled. Who was this woman? Whoever she was, she was certainly getting things organized. Soon after her first appearance he saw her cleaning the upstairs windows, leaning out to polish the outside glass. Surely a visitor wouldn't bother to do that?

The week after she arrived — the last in April — he saw her standing on the pavement one afternoon, hands on hips, overseeing the work of a brawny man in overalls. He clipped the shaggy hedge to chest height and reduced the lovely big-branched trees that had latticed the upstairs windows to ugly, squat soldiers with amputated limbs. Now Sam could see that there was a front porch, and that the front door was green. He no longer experienced the pleasant surprise of seeing Mr Reader pop out of the gap in the hedge like a magician's rabbit; now he could observe him coming out of the porch door and walking down the front path.

Though they were inhabiting the same house, Sam only saw the two together once. Mr Reader came down the front path one morning as usual, but then paused halfway along and looked back. The dark lady swelled out of the narrow porch door and waved a black umbrella. She pointed it at the sky, where two darkish clouds shadowed one patch of an otherwise cloudless sky. There seemed to be a bit of an argument but the woman won, for the old man finally took the proffered umbrella before retracing his steps to the gate. How shrunken he looked beside the huge woman. His face was most particularly sour as he walked out the gate that morning.

Sam christened the woman Sybil — a suitably forbidding name. He decided that she was Mr Reader's elder sister. Unmarried, because no man would have her, she'd been a wardress in Holloway Prison. Sam didn't know Holloway but he did know Wandsworth. He had clear memories of that formidable building — with its great outer wall topped by vicious spikes and barbed wire — standing four-square with its blind windows staring sightlessly at the nursery across the road where his parents had regularly bought plants for their small suburban garden. As a small boy he had been both fascinated and repelled by the place. Sybil awakened similar feelings, and so Sam linked the two. Why had she come to live with her brother? She must have been sacked for some misdeed; probably mistreating prisoners. Now that she had forced herself upon her poor brother, Sam was sure that the old man was visibly shrinking.

As the spring weather drew people out of their homes, so Jessica now made regular appearances in the overgrown garden, always in the afternoons. She hung out the washing, cleaned windows — window-cleaning seemed to be a disease, like chicken pox — and started to organize the garden. Sam was amazed at how hard she worked; he imagined her soft, girlish hands becoming calloused with blisters. She mowed, cut and clipped, trundling great piles of leaves and branches to the overgrown end of the garden in a large metal wheelbarrow. She dug with a spade and fork which were clearly too heavy for her, and too long. He was saddened and indignant to see her waste her energy this way; the garden looked much nicer before, all wild and jungly.

Who was her keeper? What sort of person would force a girl of Sam's age to slave like this? And what horrors did Jessica have to face in those long mornings when she never appeared?

At the end of April Sam witnessed two important events on the hill.

First, Mr Reader disappeared. At first Sam thought he might have changed his job. Perhaps he was leaving home earlier, before Sam's pre-breakfast viewing, or later, after Mrs Hooper had arrived. So on Friday, Mrs Hooper's day off, Sam remained glued to his binoculars, on and off, from 7.30 until 10.00. He saw Sybil marching out of the gate a little before ten, but no sign of her brother. And he got no further sightings of Mr Reader that evening, nor over the weekend. Was he ill? Dying? Dead, perhaps? Had she bumped him off? Being his only living relative, she would inherit the house and any money he might have saved, probably quite a lot. Sam doubted whether the little bookseller had ever spent much on himself or his home; he was obviously a bit of a miser, wearing tatty clothes and digging things out of the dustbin when he lived in a grand house like that. Sam was worried. Should he send an anonymous letter to the police? He did nothing, of course, and his feelings over the next days veered between anger with Sybil, sorrow for Mr Reader, and a faint hope that he was simply ill and would reappear in a day or so.

The second event was more dramatic, and tipped the scales of Sam's interest firmly to No. 7. It was on the afternoon of the first Friday in May, a lovely warm day. Jessica was in the garden as usual, not working for once, but sitting on the lowest branch of the spreading cedar tree at the side of the garden near Mr Reader's adjoining fence. She was gently swinging on it — he could see her white socks and strap shoes disappearing into the uncut grass and then bobbing up again. He could not see her face, screened by the foliage, but imagined that her eyes were closed. Maybe she was dreaming of a time before — when she was free and happy. He was so mesmerized by the steady rhythm of her feet gliding up and down that he did not see the old woman, until Jessica's reaction indicated that something had interrupted her thoughts. Her feet suddenly slipped down, on the upward swing; she fell forward off the branch on to her hands, and he saw her pale, upturned face, framed by her fringe. The woman was standing a little to the left of the tree, bent forward. She leant on a stick, and was bundled in a strange assortment of clothes, with a woollen shawl swathed over her head and shoulders. The girl picked herself up and approached the woman, who caught hold of her arm with her free hand. Still holding hard to Jessica's upper arm, she led her towards a shed, which was just visible beyond the cedar. He could not see the door; either it was blocked by the cedar, or it was round the other side. He lost sight of the two figures, and stared fixedly at the corner of the shed for what seemed like hours. Then the old woman reappeared, alone, shuffling slowly past the shed, round the cedar towards the side door.

He now saw her face clearly, framed by the shawl. It was very lined, like a dried prune; the nose was hawkish, and below the nose — Sam shuddered — a parody of a mouth. One side reached up to the left nostril, the other sloped down, so that her face seemed fixed in a ghastly grin. Her left hand was concealed in the folds of her shawl; the other gripped the handle of her stick, humped and clawlike. He tracked her course, grimly fascinated, until the last fold of her shawl, trail of the longish skirt, vanished through the side door. Then he panned the binoculars back to the cedar and the shed. No Jessica.

"What's she done to her?" he cried. "She must have locked her in the shed." He knocked his fist helplessly against his window. Pitch dark. Must and dust. No air to breathe nor room to move. Cobwebs and creepy crawlies. Again he knocked on the glass.

"Poor Jessica. Oh, what can I do?"

He turned from the window and slipped the glasses from his neck, dropping them on to his bed. Blinking hot tears, he stumbled from his bedroom, pocketed his door key, and let himself out of the flat. If he couldn't help her, then he couldn't watch.

Stepping out of the lift, he walked across the grassed court and up the path that led to the park, his neck and shoulders thrust forward as if he was bent on getting somewhere fast. He was not there to see the girl step lightly past the shed, a scythe balanced on one shoulder. Did not see her, awkwardly at first, then with growing confidence, swing the scythe in flat arcs, raising a light rain of grass.

Eight

Mr Forbes continued to visit the library, out of habit, after Mrs Butts moved in. But gradually it occurred to him that there was no longer any need to bestir himself in this way. Mrs Butts now did the shopping, and the first delivery of brand-new books from Grove's — books with shiny, firm bindings and unfingered pages, on whose fly leaves he could sign his own name — gave him a delightful sense of ownership. These were *his* books, not the public's.

He found Mrs Butts in the kitchen, mopping the floor. "I have much reading to do," he told her. "I must not be disturbed. Bring me, each day, a light breakfast at nine, dinner at seven. Lunch is of little consequence; a good apple and some cheese will do."

At seven o'clock that evening, Mrs Butts carried his supper tray to the door of his sitting room and, balancing it carefully on one brawny arm, knocked smartly with the other. On receiving no reply, she pushed the door open with one hip and walked in. Mr Forbes was not there.

"Seven, he said," she muttered. "And him not here." She hovered a moment, undecided, as if she hoped that his meagre form might materialize out of the battered armchair by the fireside. With a slight shrug, she returned to the kitchen and placed his plate under the grill.

She was roused from her own supper in the kitchen by a regular banging which seemed to come from the first floor. She stomped crossly up the stairs and traced the sound to Mr Forbes' bedroom. He was sitting up in bed, propped on many pillows, and was banging the floor repeatedly with a twisted walking stick. Pulled down over his head was the terrible tea cosy.

"I abhor unpunctuality," he complained. "It is now 7.17, and I have no dinner."

Mrs Butts had more sense than to argue. Silently, her mouth a grim line, she fetched his dinner and placed it on his bedside table, first removing an ashtray littered with smelly tobacco and two pipes.

Tucking his napkin into the frayed neck of the Fair Isle pullover that Ethel had knitted for his thirty-fourth birthday, Mr Forbes balanced the plate of fish pie on his knees. He drew an open book, which was lying on the faded yellow eiderdown, nearer to his side, and placed it upon the edge of a pillow that had fallen askew, tenderly stroking the pages flat with one hand. Mrs Butts saw the plate tip gently, and watched the pie juice trickle down the eiderdowned hillock of the old man's knees.

"Will that be all, sir?" she stiffly enquired.

Mr Forbes, engrossed in his book, nodded, absently drawing a forkful of pie towards the approximate area of his mouth.

Mrs Butts withdrew. Before she continued her own meal, she chalked up on the slate by the door, below: "POTS 6 LB; TABLE, 1, SUTIBLE FOR BED"

It soon became all too clear that her eccentric employer had retired — to bed. Mrs Butts received any instructions for the day when she brought him his breakfast on a tray at nine. At first, Mr Forbes outlined the evening's menu: "I suggest corned beef hash, this evening, Mrs Butts." "Fillet of plaice; that will do nicely, with plenty of lemon. And pancakes. Yes." But gradually that, too, lapsed. As the old man's bed groaned under the weight of accumulating books, his mind became laden with the weight of new information, and the boundaries between what was, and what is, became confused. "A suckling pig," he murmured to Mrs Butts one morning, "coated with mellifluous honey, and stuffed with a partridge." He was deep in a social history of the Tudor period.

Mrs Butts sniffed, cautiously moving two large volumes to one side of the bed to make room for the little invalid table she had bought for his meals. "Pork chops," she interpreted, "with apple sauce."

In addition to the cooking, shopping and housework, she posted his letters, mostly addressed to a Grove's Bookshop and the Midland Bank, cashed his cheques, and visited the library on his behalf once a week. Being of a solitary disposition, she didn't much mind the lack of visitors. If she felt the need for a chat, there was the young man who helped with the garden and odd jobs, the pleasant delivery fellow from Grove's Bookshop, and occasional afternoon visits by bus to an old friend who lived in a village a few miles outside Worple. On the whole, she found her new position most satisfactory; her employer didn't bother her, nor she him. Though his manner was brusque, he paid her well, and seemed to eat her plain but substantial meals with relish. She approved of a good appetite.

One thing, however, she decided she was not prepared to tolerate.

Having delivered his breakfast tray, she stationed herself, with arms folded, at the foot of his bed.

He swilled noisily at his tea, and turned a page.

She coughed, delicately placing her large hand in front of her mouth.

He lowered his cup and took a noisy bite from his toast.

She coughed again.

Placing his toast on his saucer, Mr Forbes raised his head and eyed her severely. "Well?"

"I pride myself, sir, on keeping a good home."

"Yes indeed, Mrs Butts, I should think so. That is why I have employed you."

"This room, sir, is a disgrace. How am I to clean it when you are always in it? And the smoke is something terrible."

He supped again, noisily, at his tea, and lowered the cup with a clatter. "You are at liberty to clean in here once a week," he conceded, "but you are not to meddle with my books."

Mrs Butts was not satisfied. "There is the matter of the bed. The sheets have not been aired or cleaned. And," she added emphatically, "there is a bathroom along the landing which is not hardly used."

Mr Forbes whinnied, and his thin, melancholy face twisted about a bit. That, thought Mrs Butts, is what he chooses to call a laugh.

"Little used, you say?" Mr Forbes whinnied again. "Very well. I shall give the bathroom practice every Friday morning, when you may do what you think necessary in here. But you are not to disarrange my books, Mrs Butts. I insist that you replace them *exactly* where you find them. Any disarrangement," and here his eyes gleamed maliciously, "and I shall bid farewell to the bathroom for ever."

"Very good, sir," said Mrs Butts. As she clumped downstairs she muttered, "Disarranged. Humph. There's no arrangement there as I can see."

Mr Forbes got the idea after reading an article in the *Daily Despatch*. A Mr White and his wife had unearthed a box of papers while clearing out their loft: nineteenth-century household receipts, diaries, and rather sentimental poems by a clearly bored young woman whose thoughts were anywhere but on the household tasks with which she should, presumably, have been occupied. For some days after reading the article, Mr Forbes found it difficult to concentrate on the books that littered his eiderdown. He felt piqued that everything he read must be shared with the nameless other readers. How pleasant it would be, he thought, to read something that no one else had read — something that had not been published, perhaps hidden away for years and years, gathering dust, until he discovered it and reintroduced it to the light of day.

The idea became an obsession. He dreamed of finding boxes of valuable manuscripts hidden under the floorboards, or gathering dust in the attic. Banging authoritatively on the bedroom floor with his stick, he summoned Mrs Butts to his bedside one morning and instructed her to spring-clean the house.

"I've done that," said Mrs Butts huffily.

"Did you find any boxes?" enquired Mr Forbes.

"Boxes *and* boxes," she replied.

"What was in the boxes?"

"*Old* slippers, *old* clothes, all sorts of junk." Mrs Butts wrinkled her nose with distaste.

"Any papers?"

"*Old* papers, too."

"Where are these papers now?"

"I threw them all out, sir, like you said." Mr Forbes groaned. He rolled out of bed and stood quivering on the bare boards in his stocking feet. "You disposed of old papers?" What might he have lost? He calmed down a little when further questioning revealed that the papers she mentioned were all newspapers. "Nothing written down, sir," Mrs Butts assured him.

But Mr Forbes was not yet ready to give up. "We must clear out the attic," he said.

He put on his flattened bedroom slippers — "like kippers" sniffed Mrs Butts — and his faded brown dressing-gown, and flip-flapped up the ladder, which they had unearthed from the cellar. For three days the two of them crawled from one end of the attic to the other, bent double to avoid the rafters, by the light of a torch and an old paraffin lantern. They found a great many spiders, one dead mouse, broken furniture and other odds and ends, but no papers.

"Well then," thought Mr Forbes, as he snuggled back into bed, "I shall advertise."

Mrs Hooper had encouraged Sam to read newspapers — local and national — to broaden his general knowledge. He needed little persuasion; he enjoyed reading them.

He was intrigued one day by a strange advertisement in the *Worple Gazette*:

> **COLLECTOR** welcomes receipt of ORIGINAL and UNPUBLISHED manuscripts, with historical, tragical or mysterious content. Payment negotiable. Apply Box 2110, Worple

"Mum. Do manuscripts have to be old?" he asked.

"No. Manuscript just means something written by hand. Why?"

"Does it *have* to be written by hand?"

"Well, *manus* means hand in Latin. In the past things were always written by hand. Now, of course, with typewriters and word processors, people don't usually bother. So manuscript can also mean simply 'unpublished' or 'unprinted'."

Sam wondered about the advertisement. Would typed pages do? His handwriting was awful — he was constantly being pulled up for it.

Over the next fortnight, he spent a good deal of his afternoons writing feverishly. Later, at times when he was alone in the flat, he painstakingly converted his illegible scrawl into fairly legible type on his mother's portable typewriter, using his two index fingers. At last he had assembled five typescript pages. Again using the typewriter, he then composed the following letter:

15 Mullet Court
Park Hill Road
Worple

31st May

Dear Sir,
I inclose a typescript of a story.
It is not a manuscript because tthe
hand writing is r ather illegable.
But it is original.
I hope you enjoy it.

Yourssincerely

Sam Leonard

Having read the letter through carefully, Sam changed the "Dear Sir" to "Dear Sir or Madam" since the advertisement gave no indication of the sex of the collector. He also crossed out "Sam Leonard" and inserted "S.L. Esquire" instead. He retyped the letter, folded it, together with the five typescript pages, into a buff envelope he had snitched from his mother's desk, neatly stuck a first-class stamp on the right-hand corner, and took the envelope down the hill to the nearest post-box.

Nine

Mr Forbes was disappointed. Somehow he had expected that his advertisement would have evoked a stream of response. But nothing came.

It was not until nearly three weeks after placing the advertisement that the interesting letter arrived. Brief, and oddly spelled, it was signed mysteriously "S.L. Esquire", and had a Worple address. Enclosed with the letter were five pages of typescript. The typist was clearly an amateur, for the spacing was irregular and there were many mistypings and crossings-out.

Mr Forbes settled himself comfortably against his pillows and began to read.

The story was about a girl called Jessica who travelled by train to stay with an unknown great-aunt. It was not clear why she came, nor where she came from. On disembarking, laden with luggage, she collided with an old lady on the platform.

> " 'Mind where you're going, careless child,' croaked the old lady in a muffled voice. She turned and Jessica saw a pair of sharp black eyes in crackled eyelids peering out of shawls. 'Have you seen a girl step off this train with a label saying Jessica Tunnings? My eyes aren't as good as they used to be.'
>
> 'I am Jessica,' she replied, 'and you are Great-Aunt Jean, I bet.'
>
> 'Don't bet,' rasped Great-Aunt Jean. 'If you bet at your age you have the makings of a criminal.' "

Mr Forbes guffawed. How rum!

Jessica and the great-aunt — clearly an unpleasant character — trudged on foot out of the town and up on to bleak moorland. Mr Forbes doubted whether an old woman with a stick and a small girl with a great deal of luggage could have managed such a journey, but he enjoyed the vigorous descriptions and grudgingly allowed for such a thing as "poetic licence". They arrived at last at a gloomy mansion, that

> "loomed on top of the lonely crag, a great slab of stone with gaping windows and tangled growth all about. Beyond a high stone wall Jessica could see one other house, staggering out of a great pile of undergrowth and encircled by a huge, shaggy hedge like a pallisade.
>
> 'Here we are at Murky House,' said Great-Aunt Jean."

Murky House was an uncomfortable place. There was no electric light; candles and tinder boxes were employed. There followed a description of flickering shadows and unseen corners as the wretched girl was led across draughty halls. At last they came to a halt in the kitchen. The aunt turned towards Jessica,

> "Her shawl slipped to her shoulders and Jessica threw her hand to her mouth to control a scream. Her aunt had a ghastly mouth which stretched up to her left nostril and dangled down almost to her chin."

At this point the story stopped. With a snort, Mr Forbes dug his hand into the envelope, but there was nothing else there.

Puzzled, he re-read the five pages.

"Odd." He tapped his teeth thoughtfully with his finger. "Strange style. Idiosyncratic spelling. Odd story altogether. And then it just stops. No title. No explanation." He re-read the letter, too, and remained as baffled as before.

He took his writing pad from his bedside table.

"Dear Sir," he wrote.

Clutching the ten pound note in disbelief, Sam read the neatly written letter out of which the money had slipped.

"Please accept the enclosed as remuneration for the story you sent me. I should be interested to learn why it is incomplete. If you find anything else, I should much like to acquire it. I am yours, most sincerely, A.F."

"Ten pounds," breathed Sam. "A.F. must be quite rich."

He worked hard for Mrs Hooper in the mornings and, after she'd left and he had prepared lunch for himself and his mother, he got his homework out of the way so that he was free to use his binoculars, and to write. Mrs Leonard, assuming that in the long hours he holed himself up in his bedroom he was doing his homework, became concerned for his health.

"You must play, too," she advised him. "A growing boy needs exercise and fresh air."

Sam smiled, and agreed. He made a point of going out for about an hour most afternoons to keep her happy. He discovered a tall oak tree up the hill in the park behind the council flats where he had as good a view of the houses on the hill as he had from his balcony. From there, perched on a broad fork with no fear of being disturbed, he watched Sybil, Jessica and — on her rare forays into the garden — the aunt.

He was surprised, on several occasions, to see a van draw up outside Number Six, with Grove's Bookshop printed on the side in large letters. A flat-faced man with a square haircut staggered up the front path with a box, presumably containing books. These were received by Sybil, who sometimes ushered the man inside for a good half-hour. What was she up to? Had she, then, taken over the running of Mr Reader's bookshop herself? Sam's suspicions as to Sybil's motives for coming to Worple were now reinforced. Later, he would use some of this information in his story.

He battered on his mother's typewriter in the half to three-quarters of an hour between Mrs Hooper's departure and his mother's return from the solicitors' office. Regular practice made him faster and more accurate. So as not to alert his mother, he bought paper, envelopes and stamps with some of his pocket money, now augmented by what he had earned.

Mr Forbes received the second instalment of the Jessica story a week after the first.

He was in a bad temper on Monday morning. The night had been hot and sultry. He had tossed off his yellow eiderdown, then his three blankets. Still unable to sleep, he had spent half an hour grappling with the window. The catch had rusted up and he had to hunt for a hammer and some oil. But any air seemed to have been sucked up into the troposphere; the window, open at last, yawned at him vindictively, soaking his already damp pyjamas with its hot breath. He must at some point have fallen asleep, for he was woken by a loud bang. It was bucketing down outside. Rolls of thunder bounced across the dawn sky like stones across a corrugated roof, and the wildly flapping curtains had dark streaks where the rain had drenched them. Having slammed the window shut, Mr Forbes tussled with the pile of bedclothes on the floor, and heaved them back on to his bed.

Wrapping his dressing-gown round his shoulders, he tried to concentrate on his book, but hc found Henry the Eighth tiresome, and Ann Boleyn more so; "spoiled little trollop," he hissed. He tossed the heavy book into a fold of his eiderdown, and frustratedly banged his pillows about. When she brought in his breakfast tray, Mrs Butts thought that he looked like a plucked, trussed turkey, surrounded by sage and onion stuffing. "Terrible night," she said. "Shall I sort you out?"

She took hold of a corner of the eiderdown, but let it fall when her employer snapped, "Leave it be! I'll have my breakfast in peace."

She later walked down to the town to do some shopping. When she got back she noticed a letter on the hall floor, and placed it on the hall table. She wasn't going to risk another snap from the old dog upstairs. She took it up to him with his lunch tray.

He snatched it from her, nearly upsetting the tray, and glowered at the envelope.

"When did you get this?" He flapped it under her nose as she bent over his bed to lower the little bed table into position.

"This morning."

"About time," he snarled, and eagerly he tore it open.

"Some people don't know their manners," said Mrs Butts decisively as she edged round the end of the bed. Mr Forbes chose not to hear.

S.L.'s letter did not enlighten Mr Forbes as to the source of the story. It was as short and uninformative as the first one.

> I enclose some more typescript pages.
> I hope you like them.
> Yours sincerely,
>
> S.L. Esquire

In these pages, the hapless Jessica was forced to work for her terrible aunt from dawn to dusk, sweeping, polishing, scrubbing, laundering. She was also ordered to clear the land round the house and plant vegetables — a hard task on the stony moorland soil. "One hot afternoon," read Mr Forbes,

> "she staggered between the outside tap and the vegetable plot with a heavy metal watering can over and over again; then she limped across to a huge tree by the wall, and stood, panting,

beneath its cool, spreading branches. One lower branch curved down almost to the ground. Jessica rested against it and it gently bowed under her weight. She jumped lightly onto the branch and, closing her eyes blissfully, swung up, down, up, down, in a dreamy trance. Her long blonde hair hung over her face like a thick curtain.

'Idle brat!'

The voice so startled her that she fell off the branch and landed heavily on her outstretched hands. A strong, twisted hand pinched her arm and pushed her towards the garden shed.

'There's a place for layabouts,' snarled Great-Aunt Jean, writhing her deformed mouth. Slowly she pushed the gasping girl towards the shed. Still grasping her arm, she ordered her to remove the ring of keys that jangled at her waist.

'This one,' the old hag hissed, pointing to a large rusty key. Jessica obediently took the key and fumbled with the heavy padlock. At last it snapped open. She was thrust into the yawning doorway and the door clanged shut. A jangle of keys. Silence.

It was dark inside and musty. The smallest movement made her touch cold metal with sharp edges, and she felt the sticky fingers of cobwebs on her face and cold bare arms. She crouched on the damp earth floor and wound her arms tightly round her knees. There was no sound except her own breathing, and the darkness was so thick that it seemed like a wall. She was spinning in a wind tunnel. She gulped cold air which battered on her mouth and chest like something solid, too thick to breathe. The darkness raced towards her and pressed on her. She was crushed by the hands and feet of crawling aliens. Frantically she tried to push them away, and as she struggled with the writhing shapes they fell apart, dropping in soft lumps like putty. The silence was ripped by screams, as she banged against the locker door.

'Mummy, get me out,' she screamed. 'Daddy, Daddy!'

"Confound it," yelled Mr Forbes. "It's stopped again!" The

typing did, indeed, suddenly come to an end half-way down the fourth page.

Gathering up the typescript pages, Mr Forbes shook them angrily. "If it's money S.L. is after, then I'm not such a fool," he growled. Indignantly he wrote a letter to him.

Sam was appalled when he got A.F.'s second letter. "I may be an old man, but I am not a foolish one. I will not send another penny until you send me the rest of the story."

So A.F. thought he was a money-grubber. But how could he send the end of the story when there was no end as yet? He could just stop corresponding with the old man, but Sam wanted to write — very much. In his story he could communicate the things he could not share with the adults in his life, and the story must be read by someone to exist. He wrote one letter after another to A.F., and tore each of them up. He couldn't seem to get them right.

Days passed and Sam had posted nothing back. He felt, somehow, as if he was betraying the people on the hill. So long as he failed to write about them, their lives would be frozen. Jessica must toil endlessly in the house and garden, with no hope of escape, and Mr Reader was fading away — a dying prisoner in his own home. Eventually, desperate to break the deadlock, Sam got out of bed in the early hours of one morning, and wrote several pages about Mr Reader and Sybil. He typed some of these in the half-hour between his mother leaving for work and Mrs Hooper's arrival, and the rest before Mrs Leonard came home for lunch. Still stumped as to what to write in his covering letter, he simply scrawled on the top of the first typed sheet, "It's happening now. It can't end." He ran down the hill to the pillar box, and felt a surge of relief as he pushed the envelope into the slot.

*

When the days passed and nothing further arrived from S.L., Mr Forbes began to regret his letter. "Stupid old miser, that's what I am," he rebuked himself. "What's ten pounds to me, anyway?"

On several occasions he placed his writing pad on his knee and tried to write to S.L. But what could he say without first having to apologize? Apologies came hard to Mr Forbes. He felt restless and irritable, and had difficulty in concentrating on any one of his books. Often he took up the two sheaves of typescript that he kept on his bedside table, and re-read them. They were, he remarked all over again, poorly typed, poorly spelled, and none too well-written; too many adjectives, and the story itself was full of holes. Why, for instance, did Jessica have to stay with her aunt in the first place? And surely, isolated on the moor as they were, someone would have to go to town to buy provisions. Why couldn't Jessica simply run away then? Despite all these weaknesses, Mr Forbes found the story compelling. He wanted to know more about Jessica, and more about S.L.

If Mr Forbes had had any experience of children he might have deduced that the Jessica story had been written by a child. But he knew no children, and his recollections of his own childhood were distinctly hazy. His elder sister, Ethel, was the only child he had known well, since his brothers were several years his senior and had always treated him with mild indifference. Close in age, and both sent to the small local school, they had kept their own company. Ethel had always seemed to him a little woman. Indeed, he remembered his mother calling her just that when she was quite a little pig-tailed thing. Mr Forbes recognized only that the story was different in some way. He had read nothing else like it. Besides, it was his; nobody else had read it.

When Sam's next sheaf of typescript pages was delivered to his bedside by Mrs Butts, Mr Forbes was delighted. The fact that this story had nothing to do with Jessica — contained no mention of her, in fact — did not worry him. Instead, it was all about a lonely old recluse called Mr Reader who lived in a rambling house on a moor and owned an antiquarian bookshop. Lonely moors seemed to be the fashion, grinned Mr Forbes. The old man's peaceful existence was shattered by the unwelcome arrival of his sister.

The style of writing was definitely S.L.'s. The typeface was the same as the Jessica story, and the postmark was again Worple. Mr Forbes understood now that S.L. had to be the author of the story, or stories. "It's happening now. It can't end" — scrawled at the top of the first sheet in leaky biro — presumably meant that the author was still writing the story. He was a witness to the actual act of creation! How strange that the author should be prepared to let him see the story before its completion. And how exciting. Maybe he — Archie Forbes — could in some way influence the direction of the author's pen.

He was puzzled by "It can't end." Perhaps what the author meant was, "It can't end yet, because I haven't written it." Well, he would help S.L. to write it, and finish it. He would set himself up as the writer's patron — encouraging him, correcting him and, of course, keeping him from starvation.

Gratified and excited, the old man wrote to S.L., enclosing two ten pound notes.

Box 2110
Worple
27th June

Dear S.L.,
I was most gratified to receive your story about Mr. Reader and his terrible

sister, Sybil. At first I was perplexed; what had happened to Jessica? But I think I see now. Mr Reader also lives in an isolated house on a moor, and 'over the high stone wall, half-hidden by trees, brambles and undergrowth, is another grim building'. Might this be Murky House, I wonder? Are the lives of Jessica and Mr Reader to be linked in some way?

I understand, now, why you have sent your tale in instalments. You are, of course, the author, and I your sole reader. Privileged as I am to be your confidant, might I offer a few words of advice?

Take care not to use too many adjectives. You must take more pains with your plot, finding valid reasons for the events that take place. Why, for instance, does Jessica have to stay with her great-aunt? Why does she not run away? She's a young lady of spirit, after all. I hope you will ensure that Jessica finally regains her freedom.

I trust you will take my advice in good part, and consider me a friend.

I look forward to the next instalment. In the meantime, please accept the enclosed for this, and the previous, instalment.

I am yours, most sincerely,
Archibald Forbes

P.S. Perhaps I might know your name?

When he handed the letter to Mrs Butts, he looked very pleased with himself. "It's a fine day, Mrs Butts," he said, almost jovially. "Take a walk in the sunshine, and I should be grateful if you could post this on your way."

Mrs Butts cautiously took the letter; this was an about-turn from the crabbed old buzzard's recent mood. She overcame her natural reticence to enquire, "Did you get something good in the post, then, sir?"

Her employer grinned and rubbed his hands. "I have got myself a protégé, Mrs Butts," he said.

As she went downstairs with the letter, Mrs Butts wondered what dreadful thing a protergey might be. Some hideous garment or, worse still, some kind of animal, maybe a nasty reptile. "I wouldn't put it past him," she muttered. "Well, I'll not stay in this house if there's any creepy-crawlies about — money or no money."

Ten

"You seem to be getting a lot of post these days, Sam," said his mother curiously, as she handed him a neatly addressed envelope. She peered at it. "S.L. Esquire, indeed: what are you up to?"

"Oh, nothing, Mum," said Sam, taking the letter. "Just a friend."

"Who? What friend?"

"Kevin," Sam lied. Kevin had been a schoolfriend of his in London.

"I didn't know you'd kept up with Kevin." His mother sounded pleased. "Perhaps we could have him to stay in the summer holidays."

"Perhaps," Sam mumbled evasively. Then, looking at his watch, "Hurry up with your breakfast, Mum, or you'll be late for work."

"Cheeky devil!" laughed Mrs Leonard. But she obediently bit into her toast.

As soon as she had gone, Sam tore open the envelope. He unfolded the letter it contained, and an enclosure fell onto the floor. He glanced down. There were two brand new ten pound notes at his feet. Sam felt like Dick Whittington: the floor was paved with gold. He picked them up and savoured their crispness.

A flood of warmth surged through him, making him feel slightly dizzy. He had a vivid picture of his mother laughing across the kitchen table. He had given her such a rotten time. Still fingering the notes, he lapsed into a pleasant daydream.

In a few more weeks he could have earned enough to give his mother a grand surprise. How about a weekend away? He would slip down to the travel agents in the High Street and make enquiries. Life was really looking up for him; for them both. He felt sure of it.

Mrs Hooper arrived before Sam had a chance to read the letter. He stuffed it into his trouser pocket and grinned at his tutor. "Hello, Mrs Hooper. I'm in the mood for everything today."

She laughed. "Splendid! We'll see just how much of everything we can squeeze into a morning."

The morning sped by. Mrs Hooper was so enchanted by Sam's quickness that she lost all sense of time. They were still bent over his table, their heads close together, when Mrs Leonard let herself in. Their enthusiasm was infectious. Mrs Leonard was shown the map of an imaginary town that Sam had drawn. He had invented some amusing symbols to represent the public buildings and services. They all got involved in a noisy argument as to whether it was easier to read a map upwards or downwards, and Sam's mother admitted that she could only follow southward directions by turning the map upside down. Sam teased her about her "left-right bump": "If Mum says 'Turn right', the safest thing is to turn left," he explained to Mrs Hooper.

It was nearly one o'clock, so Mrs Hooper was invited to stay to lunch and, as it was a glorious day, they decided to take a walk afterwards.

Sam had completely forgotten A.F.'s letter. He got a fit of the sneezes as a result of their walk in the fields above the park and, hunting through his pockets for a handkerchief, his fingers closed round the letter, still stuffed deep into his trouser pocket. He was still unable to read it, however, as he and his mother decided to walk down to the High Street to do some shopping.

His chance came when his mother was preparing supper. It was much longer than previous letters, and he was confused by it. He read it through several times. He was flattered that Archibald Forbes (Archibald? What a name!) should call him an author; he hadn't thought of himself as one. But for the most part the letter unsettled him. The old man seemed to think that Sam could control the lives of the people who lived on the hill. But how could he? They were not puppets and he the puppeteer. He simply watched them and recorded what he saw.

He folded the letter several times and stuffed it back in his pocket. He had a frightening sense of unreality. If it was all a story, and he the author, then the characters had been invented. They weren't real.

Feeling slightly sick, he hurried to his room and removed his binoculars from their case. He went out on to the balcony and focussed the binoculars on Number Seven. Jessica was in the garden. Yes — she was quite definitely, solidly, there, trundling to and fro with the large metal wheelbarrow. Mr Forbes was a silly old idiot. He watched her make a great heap of garden rubbish at the back of the garden where Mr Reader's fence adjoined the property. Then she went indoors, and returned with a wad of newspaper under one arm. These she fisted into balls and meticulously buried them at strategic points in the heap of rubbish. He watched her light matches and ignite the paper balls. Then she stood back, with her hands on her hips, watching the dry cuttings catch alight. Apparently satisfied, she turned away, and started hoeing in the vegetable patch. Sam swivelled his binoculars, now to Jessica, now to the fire; sometimes whispers of bonfire smoke drifted in front of her, and made her swaying form with its sheaf of blonde hair shimmer and almost disintegrate. The tongues of flame lapped higher and higher, and Sam imagined the tang of woodsmoke in his nostrils and seemed to hear the crack and snap as a twig exploded, and the sizzle of roasting sap. The motion of fire and girl seemed to complement one another, like partners in a dance, and Sam felt excited. Jessica's activity became more vigorous as the spate of the fire increased, until each seemed to be vying with the other. Set against a backdrop of a golden evening light, the scene was theatrical.

Suddenly, Jessica swung the hoe above her shoulder and ran towards the fire. She brought its head down on the flames then raised it again, and again swung down. At first Sam had the strange feeling that the girl was engaging in some kind of ritualistic dance, but then it dawned on him that she was frantically struggling to keep the fire down. The flames reached, now, high above her head, and were angling to the right, towards the partition fence. That, too, burst into flame.

Stunned, Sam willed Jessica to win her lonely battle. When a second figure — a small, dark, scurrying thing — entered the circle of his vision, he saw it simply as an addition to Jessica's army. So bright was the glare of the flames that Sam did not notice that the last light had faded from the hillside. Now there were four dark shapes flitting to and fro in front of the flames, and between the tap by the side door and the fire. In the confusion of bright light, dark shadows and frantic activity, Sam concluded that a hosepipe was being fixed up. He realized, now, who the other figures were. The small, bent shape was Jessica's aunt, the large one Sybil, and the thin one Mr Reader himself, in a billowing dressing-gown. So the old man was alive and kicking after all. It was strange, and moving, to see all of them together, fighting a common enemy.

The hose had been unravelled, and the four figures were scurrying back towards the inferno. The jet of water seemed to be having no effect. For as it flattened the patch of fire upon which it was aimed, other areas spurted up as if to counterbalance, like someone bouncing on an airbed. Almost imperceptibly, however, the accumulative damp must have been reducing the heat at the centre, for all at once the golden tower climbed less high, and stretched less wide, until the fence was quite doused and the fire was confined to the area of its source.

As if determined to have its final fling, a last great tongue of flame shot out in the direction of the four silhouetted figures, followed by a rain of sparks. In that last sweep of light, Sam saw the hunched form of the old woman fling itself upon the girl, whose golden hair, caught in the light, was unmistakable. She struck Jessica several times, and the girl, with her hands raised to shield her face, reeled back from the fire, then seemed to fall. The bulk of Mr Reader's sister joined the two struggling figures, and she, too, attacked Jessica. At that moment the last flicker of the fire was extinguished. Sam could make out nothing clearly; saw only a confused sort of huddle moving towards the side of the house. For a second, by the light from the side door, he saw that the two women were half-pulling, half-carrying Jessica between them, and that she struggled violently. Then the door closed behind them.

Where was Mr Reader?

"Coward!" yelled Sam. "You cowardly old slime! Why didn't you help her? How could you let them beat her!" His binoculars were steamed up with angry tears.

"Sam. What is it? What's the matter?"

His mother turned him to face her. "What's happened?"

Sam pressed his face into her shoulder and sobbed. He let her lead him into the sitting-room and sit him on the sofa.

When at last he had quietened down, she asked him again to tell her what was wrong.

How could he explain? How could he tell her that just across the valley lived a girl who was severely ill-treated by her cruel aunt? She wouldn't believe him.

"Nightmare," he hiccoughed. "I had another nightmare — about Dad."

Her startled eyes met his. "But you weren't asleep. You were standing on the balcony."

"A waking nightmare," Sam said.

"Tell me about it," said his mother.

Sam told her how he saw a great fire, and a crowd of people dancing round it, and on the fire a guy. And the guy was his father.

"Oh, Sam," said Mrs Leonard softly. "Poor Sam."

Guiltily, Sam edged out of his mother's arms.

"I'm okay now, Mum," he said. "I think I'll go to my room for a bit."

Sam paced up and down, treading a triangle between his wardrobe, his bed and the door. What was happening to Jessica now? Was she being beaten black and blue by those horrible women? Or locked in a cupboard, alone in the dark? Perhaps he should tell his mother after all; maybe she would know what to do. No. Adults were so blind; too occupied with their own worries to see beyond the ends of their own noses. She would say he was exaggerating. Impatiently he chewed his nails; what should he do? A thought struck him.

He pulled out the crumpled letter and re-read it. "I hope you will ensure that Jessica finally regains her freedom." A.F. believed it was in Sam's power to help Jessica. Maybe it was. Maybe he was the only person who *could* help her.

Decisively, he took down the box in which he had stored the advertisement, his letters from A.F. and, in a neatly folded envelope, the money A.F. had sent him. He carried the box over to his bed, removed the envelope containing the money, and unfolded the notes. Then he emptied out his piggy bank. Carefully he counted the notes and coins. There were the thirty pounds from Mr Forbes, and seven pounds and sixty pence from his piggy bank. Sitting on the edge of his bed he wistfully fingered the crisp new notes. He'd never held so much money before. A real treat for his mother and himself—

that would have been so nice. But Jessica needed it more; maybe with money she would have the confidence to escape. And yet his mother deserved something, too; she worked so hard.

Mrs Leonard was worried. What was all that about? Waking nightmares? She made two cups of coffee and, too preoccupied to think of knocking on Sam's bedroom door as she usually would have done, she walked in.

He was sitting on the edge of his bed, and fanned out in his hands were several notes. Sam glanced up, startled, and guiltily thrust the notes between his thighs.

Mrs Leonard stared at her son. "Let me see those, Sam," she said.

"See what?"

"That money." She sounded grim.

"Mum! It's not what you think. I've *earned* it." Sam drew the notes out and held them tightly.

Mrs Leonard placed the two mugs on Sam's bedside table and advanced on him, both hands held out, palm-upwards. "Give it to me."

Still clutching the notes tightly, Sam drew his hands out towards his mother and spread them out with thumb and index finger like a hand of cards, so that she could see them.

"Thirty-five pounds," breathed Mrs Leonard. "How could you *earn* thirty-five pounds?"

"Writing. I wrote stories, and he paid me thirty pounds for them."

"Stories? Who? Who paid you? What is all this about, Sam?"

Sam blurted out an explanation — the advertisement in the papers, the letters, the money.

His mother, totally confused, sat beside him on the bed and told him to begin again from the beginning. She questioned him carefully, read Mr Forbes' letters, read the advertisement.

"And where are these stories?" she enquired.

"Mr Forbes has got them."

"I see." Mrs Leonard got up and paced slowly up and down Sam's bedroom, her forehead creased in a worried frown. Sam, still holding the precious notes, watched her cautiously from his bed.

His mother suddenly came to a stop in the middle of the room and turned to face him.

"You'll have to give it back, Sam."

"Why?" Sam leapt indignantly from the bed. "I earned it, Mum. He likes my stories. If he wants to pay for them, why shouldn't he? I didn't ask for any money. He just sent it."

"It's still not right. Thirty-five pounds for —. That's a lot of money for a pensioner. Look —." She touched Sam's chin but he angrily shook her off. "He's probably a bit . . . ." How was she to explain her gut reaction to him? "I don't think he realises you're a child, Sam. He's probably a bit — eccentric. He *needs* that money, for heating, food. You've got to return the money. You really can't keep it."

As his mother stumbled to find an explanation for her confused feelings, Sam experienced an anger that was new to him. It was like measles without the spots; sudden spasms of heat followed by a chilling sensation. What business was it of hers? She had no right to barge into his room without knocking. No right to his money — for it was undeniably his. But he knew her; saw the firm line of her mouth and chin. She really meant what she said; he'd have to return the money.

"All right." His voice was icy. "I'll pay it back. But *I'll* do it; not you. It's my business."

"Yes. Yes, all right. Of course it would be best if you returned it. But I'd like to see your letter. It might be best if I enclosed a letter with yours, explaining things. We mustn't upset the poor old man." She looked hard at her son, trying to make him out. "You do understand, Sam? It's not that —. I'm sure your stories are very good, but . . . ."

"I understand." Sam turned his back on her. He gathered up the coins which were heaped on his bed and placed them, the notes, the letters and the advertisement back in the box. "I'll write to Mr Forbes tomorrow." He walked over to his wardrobe and replaced the box on the top shelf. Fastidiously, he shuffled it about, until it lay just so in the corner. Then he made a show of tidying that, and other, shelves.

Mrs Leonard watched his back for a moment, wanting to say or do something to break the silence. Was she perhaps wrong? She opened her mouth as if about to speak; then, apparently changing her mind, shut it, and the door.

As soon as Sam heard the door shut, he turned away from the cupboard and back to his bed, where he sat, tight-lipped and deep in thought.

He felt a crying urge to communicate his anger and confusion to someone. Sliding from his bed, he took down his notebook and began to write furiously. He was still scribbling when his mother called him to supper. He stowed his notebook in the box with the letters, and picked up the book he was currently reading from his bedside table.

He brought the book to the kitchen and read throughout the meal. Normally, Mrs Leonard would have objected to such antisocial behaviour, but she realized how disappointed Sam must be feeling and let him be. Hopefully, he would be more approachable by tomorrow, and they could talk things through then.

After supper, he silently helped her to clear the table, and then returned to his room to "finish some homework". At 8.45 Mrs Leonard suggested he have a bath. She heard the water running, and a little after nine Sam came to her in the sitting room, where she was watching television, and told her he was going to bed. He absently offered her his cheek for a kiss and returned quietly to his room. During the mid-news advertisement break, she poked her head round his door. His light was out and he was asleep.

"Sleep well, Sam," she whispered, "and please try to understand."

Eleven

Sam was not asleep. He lay wide-eyed and alert, waiting impatiently for the sounds of his mother preparing to go to bed. His plans were far from clear, but of two things he was certain. He was *not* going to return the money to Mr Forbes, and he *was*, somehow, going to help Jessica to escape from her aunt's clutches. The old man had lost the right to Sam's interest. He had stood by and watched while Great-Aunt Jean and his sister had beaten Jessica mercilessly. His life was probably miserable, now that Sybil had moved in, but he deserved no better. And clearly she wasn't poisoning him, or he would not have been able to leave his bed to help put out the fire in the next-door-neighbour's garden. He could jolly well look after himself.

Sam had no idea how he was going to rescue Jessica, nor even how he would contact her, but the first thing must be to go over to the houses on the hill and keep watch. Luckily, the weather had been warm and settled.

When he heard his mother's bath running, he crept out of bed and opened his door a fraction. At last he heard the faint click as she switched off the bathroom light pull, and her feet padding along the corridor to her room. Another click as her bedroom door closed. He glanced at the dial of his illuminated watch. It was 11.36. He would wait a clear half-hour before getting out of bed. She usually read for a bit.

At precisely 12.06 he slipped out of bed, quietly closed his door, and switched on his bedside light. He put on a vest, sweatshirt, warm sweater, jeans and woollen socks — it might get quite cold out there on the hillside. In his canvas haversack he packed a spare sweater and socks, all his money, his torch and a woollen winter hat. Creeping in the dark to the bathroom, he collected a small towel (it might be useful for sitting on) and his toothbrush. In the kitchen he found his plastic drinking bottle, which he filled with lemonade. He also packed some cheddar, three apples, a packet of salt and vinegar crisps and half a packet of ginger biscuits. He shouldered his haversack, slung the binoculars round his neck, picked up his plimsolls from beside the boiler and tiptoed to the front door. He unhooked his anorak and scarf from the pegs by the door, slung them over his arm, and unlatched the front door. Well-oiled, it shut behind him without a sound. He crouched down to slip on his plimsolls, and then took the lift to the ground floor.

The court was deserted. It was a clear, chill night. Keeping close to the buildings where the shadows were deepest, he crossed one side of the court, passed between the two lower council blocks, and made his way down Park Hill Street. At the bottom of the hill, on the left, was the primary school he had briefly attended. A cat was slinking along one side of the deserted asphalt playground, and a near-full moon was reflected in one of the upper windows.

Making no sound in his sneakers and walking briskly, Sam soon reached the nearer end of Worple High Street. He crossed over, and then turned right up one of the steeply climbing narrow streets which straggled up the hill on the opposite side of the valley from the council estate.

Startled by footsteps, he darted into a dark alley that ran alongside a bookshop, called Grove's. So this was the old man's shop. With beating heart, he flattened himself against the wall. He heard a high-pitched giggle, and then a couple passed the alley entrance on their way down the hill. The young man moved silently in soft-soled shoes, the girl's high heels clattered self-consciously. As the sound of her teetering footsteps faded away, he slipped out of his hiding place, pausing a moment to peer in at the bookshop window before continuing up the hill. Maybe the old man wasn't called Mr Reader after all, but Mr Groves. And if he wasn't Mr Reader, then perhaps Sybil wasn't Sybil. And if . . . Alarmed at the direction of his thoughts, he concentrated on getting his bearings.

The road climbed steeply, curved sharply to the left, and passed a churchyard. This must be the church whose tower had formed a landmark in his binocular viewings. In that case, if he continued on up, and then worked his way to the left, he should hit a road that led to the houses on the hill. Superstitiously, he crossed the lane and passed by the churchyard on the further side, then crossed back when safely past.

When at last he came out on the upper lane, he failed at first to recognize it as the correct one. The houses at this near end had always been hidden behind some office blocks and, being smaller and semi-detached, were quite different from the larger houses at the western end. Sam continued along the lane. The semi-detached houses petered out on the upper hillside; there was a patch of rough uncultivated ground, a long, high wall with several driveway entrances, and then he was walking alongside a neatly-cut hedge. It was only when he reached the opening in the hedge for the front path that he realized he was standing in front of Number Six. The wall must conceal the first five rather grand houses in the row; from his elevated position in the tower block he would have been able to see over it. He stared curiously at the front porch, shrouded in darkness, seeing in his mind's eye the thin figure of Mr Reader, a book under his arm, walking towards him. Then, recalling the old man's betrayal of Jessica, he angrily pushed the image from his mind and passed on.

Jessica's house was also in darkness, as he had expected. It was strange to be so close. Quietly, he opened the gate and approached the front door. He stared up at the shadowy brick house. Which window was Jessica's? Was the side door locked? Most likely; and even if it were not, and he was able to find Jessica's room without being detected, he would only alarm her. Best to try and make himself known to her in daylight, perhaps while she was working in the garden. He crept round to the back of the house, to the end of the garden near the vegetable patch. There were several shrubs and a couple of largish trees up against the back fence. He pushed in among the bushes and made a snug space for himself.

Mrs Leonard was halfway through her second cup of tea and Sam had still not surfaced. Was he still sulking about the money? A little reluctantly, for she had to leave for work any minute and didn't want to start the morning with any awkwardness, she went to his room and knocked on his door.

"Come on, Sam. It's late."

There was no reply, so she opened the door. His duvet was thrown back and his wardrobe doors were wide open. She knew as she rushed from room to room of their tiny flat, calling him, that he was not there. She should have realized that something was brewing; he had taken her reaction to the repayment of the money far too calmly.

She returned to Sam's room and sat on his crumpled bed to think. Where on earth could he have gone? Silly to be theatrical; he probably hadn't run away at all. Letting herself out of the flat, she walked quickly round the court and down to the small arcade of shops on the estate. He was not there.

Running back home, she prayed that he would be there, but the flat was as empty as she had left it.

She must keep a clear head. The first thing to determine was whether he had really run away, or was just skulking somewhere to frighten her. If he'd made serious plans, he would have taken what he needed with him; he was a practical boy. He had put the money away in that box last night — if it was still there . . . .

She reached up to the top shelf, in the corner, where she'd seen him put the money. The letters and the advertisement were still in the box but the money was gone. So, too, she discovered, had his anorak, haversack — and binoculars. This was indeed serious.

Pacing nervously up and down the little hall, Mrs Leonard wondered whether she should ring the police. She picked up the local directory, then slapped it down. No. For God's sake, not the police; not yet. Questioning. Publicity. And if there really was something not quite right about the money from the old man — where would it end? She must try and find Sam herself.

Where was he likely to go? Where *could* he go? To his friend Kevin in London? He had enough money for the train fare, but surely he would realize that Kevin's parents would instantly contact her. There was no one else. The enormity of their current isolation as a family suddenly hit her. How appalling that her son should be so friendless. She should not have moved from familiar things in London; it had been cowardly to run away. "Oh, Sam. When I find you I'll make it up to you. I won't let us go on living this way."

Had he then just wandered off on his own, to nowhere, no one, in particular? A lonely, dark-eyed boy trudging along a road, or jolting in a train. Surely someone would notice him, ask questions. Or would they? Again she stared at the directory. She feverishly leafed through it and found the number for Worple police station.

"Worple Police." The man's voice sounded bored. She silently held the receiver against her ear. Her mouth felt dry. Could he hear her breathing? Panic-stricken, she banged the receiver down.

The old man. Mr? Mr Forbes. She ran into Sam's room and took down the box. It was a faint chance, but just possible, that he knew something from Sam's letters to him that she did not. On re-reading the letters she was frustrated again. There was no address, simply a post office box number. But he lived somewhere in Worple, and Worple was not such a big town.

She returned to the hall and thumbed through the directory. Forbes, Forbes, A. There were only two A. Forbes. She lifted the receiver and dialled the first of the two numbers. No reply. She replaced the receiver, then raised it again and dialled the second.

"Hello. 780-3516." A local accent. A woman.

"Er. Is Mr Forbes there, please?"

"Who is it speaking?"

"I'm Mrs Leonard. He doesn't know me but . . ."

"Could you wait a moment, please."

There was a longish wait, then the woman's voice again. "I'm afraid Mr Forbes is busy. What do you want?"

"Oh." Mrs Leonard felt betrayed. "Please. You see, he may be able to help me. It's my son. My son Sam. He's disappeared. I thought perhaps — it's silly, I know — but I thought Mr Forbes might be able to help."

There was a pause at the other end. Then the woman's voice, abrupt but not unfriendly. "Why should he be able to help? He never sees anyone nor goes anywhere. He says he doesn't know you, even."

"But I think he knows my son," she cried. "Well, not know him exactly, but his stories."

"Stories?" The woman sounded startled. "Well, just hang on, Mrs, and I'll ask."

Mrs Leonard began to feel that she'd made a mistake. This was awful. She was wasting time; she ought to talk to the police. She let her arm fall, dangling the receiver. When a faint sound issued from the phone at the level of her hip she started, and dropped it. Clumsily catching at the coiled flex, she pressed the receiver to her ear. "Hello? Hello?"

"Hello." It was the woman's voice again. "I'm sorry, Mrs. Mr Forbes is — unwell. He says he don't know you and can't help. I'm right sorry . . . Hello. Hello, are you there?"

The earpiece was pressed so hard against Mrs Leonard's ear that the woman's burr seemed to growl in the innermost part of her head. "I — I thought —" she mumbled, then realized that she was not speaking into the phone, and the woman could not possibly hear. She moved it close to her mouth, and whispered, "Thank you." Then she replaced it in its cradle.

She leaned against the wall. There was a bitter taste in her mouth. She was only jolted from her immobility by the sudden peal of the doorbell.

As she went to the door, she had, for a moment, the irrational expectation that Mr Forbes would be standing on the landing — a wheezy, slightly potty, little old man in a beret. But it was only Mrs Hooper, come to tutor Sam.

"Hello," she said breathlessly. Defensively she side-stepped, blocking the narrow doorway.

Mrs Hooper looked startled. "Oh — hello," she replied. Her ginger eyebrows flattened concernedly. "Not well?"

"No — yes. I mean . . . ." Sophie Leonard, in her confusion, knew only that she felt too bruised to take the touch of anyone else's concern. She was faintly appalled to find herself apologising to Sam's tutor with a downright lie. "Sam seemed fine last night, but is throwing quite a temperature this morning. I've popped him back into bed and he's asleep now. I tried to phone you but you must have been on your way here." How glibly she lied.

"Not to worry." Mrs Hooper gave Mrs Leonard's arm a reassuring squeeze. "I'm sure it's nothing to worry about. A lot of children are down with bugs at the moment." She hovered on the landing, and Mrs Leonard knew she ought at least to offer her a cup of tea, having come all this way for nothing.

She forced a smile. "Well, I'm awfully sorry to have dragged you over here for nothing. I'll give you a ring when he's well enough to continue his lessons."

Mrs Hooper nodded vigorously. Then she craned her thin neck forwards and peered at Sam's mother.

"Are you sure you're all right? Your eyes look rather . . . ."

"Oh, it's nothing. A slight cold."

"I am sorry. Well, I suppose I'd better be going." Stuffing her ungainly handbag under one arm, she nodded her head. "Goodbye, Mrs Leonard. Give my love to Sam."

Mrs Leonard thankfully closed the door, and leaned weakly against it. "Oh please," she whispered, "I can't stand this."

Mrs Butts replaced the receiver thoughtfully. Whoever that lady was, she was very upset. No doubt on that. What had that old crow been up to?

Mrs Butts was generally one to mind her own business, and leave others to theirs, but she also had a strong sense of justice. Something told her that in this instance her employer was being less than just, and that the unhappy lady had been wronged.

Having made her mind up, she climbed the stairs to Mr Forbes' bedroom. He glanced up from his book irritably. "What is it? You've been popping in and out all morning like a yo-yo."

She stationed herself at the foot of his bed and eyed him severely.

"You didn't ought to do that, sir," she said.

"What? What?" He slammed his book on the bedside table. "What didn't I ought — oughtn't I to do? What?"

"That poor lady," she staunchly continued. "She was right

worried about something. You should have spoken with her, sir. You should."

Mr Forbes clenched his hands and made a strange sound, something between a yell and a sneeze. "What is this idiocy, woman?" he spluttered. "Other people's worries are no concern of mine. I've never heard of the woman, or her son. She probably thought I was someone else."

Mrs Butts held her ground. "She said as you know her son. She said you know some stories. She was definite."

Mr Forbes stretched his head forwards on its scraggy neck. He really did look just like a plucked turkey, thought Mrs Butts, not for the first time.

"What stories? What's this about stories?"

"I told you, sir, the last time," said Mrs Butts patiently. "She said her son that's gone off had some stories that you knew something of. She said you might be able to help."

"Stories, she said?" Mr Forbes looked interested. "Did she mention an advertisement?" he asked, after a thoughtful pause.

"No. I don't think so."

"Maybe she read my advertisement. Perhaps she had some stories to send me." Then, impatiently, "Damn it! There was no need to bother me with telephone calls. She should send it to the special post box address."

Mrs Butts was getting lost, but one thing she hung on to. "No, sir," she corrected him. "She said you *knew* the stories. If she'd got some stories that she hadn't sent, you couldn't have *known* about them now, could you?"

They had reached temporary stalemate. The shrunken old man and his sturdy housekeeper stared at one another vindictively.

It was Mrs Butts who broke the silence. Perhaps, from her position of greater height, she felt she had the edge.

"If you've done that poor lady some wrong," she said deliberately, "then you ought to put it right."

Mr Forbes stared at her in disbelief. The large room seemed suddenly too small for the two of them. Catching hold of the nearest book, in hands shaking with indignation, he hurled it at Mrs Butts.

Silently she followed its flight across the room, to see it hit the chest of drawers with a thud, before falling to the floor. Then she turned, and with the light step that often accompanies bulky frames, walked to the door, which she closed carefully behind her. This was war.

Twelve

Sam was woken by the birds. One leg was cramped and he felt chilled. He munched an apple, some cheese and his packet of crisps, sipped some lemonade, and felt easier. It was a little after 6.15 a.m. No one would be up yet. He climbed stiffly out of the bush and wondered what to do. A bit of exercise would loosen him up and he could check the lie of the land. Leaving his haversack hidden in the bush, he pushed his way through the undergrowth alongside the back fence, which was in a state of disrepair. About two-thirds of the way along, several slats had collapsed. That would be his escape route, if it were needed.

He still felt cold, despite wearing nearly all the clothes he'd brought with him. The sky was overcast. If past form was anything to go by, Jessica was unlikely to be working in the garden until the afternoon. Either he'd have to sit tight all morning until she emerged, or he could try sneaking into the house later on, which might be risky. He decided to wait.

Returning to the bush where he had spent the night, he had nothing to do, and nothing to watch. At about 9.30 the sky darkened and the temperature dropped. Sam felt restless, cramped and hungry; this waiting made him nervous. He had another snack. Then, taking his binoculars, he crawled back through the undergrowth to the gap in the fence and climbed up, through brambles and birch, to a gorse-dotted moor. From here he could see across the valley to his council estate. It was odd to be looking the other way. He trained his binoculars on the block in which he had voluntarily incarcerated himself for so many months, and worked out which balcony was theirs. He felt a twinge of panic. Was Mum there, worrying about him, or had she gone to work without realizing he'd gone? Perhaps he should have left a note. He lowered his binoculars and deliberately concentrated his thoughts on Jessica. Mum must wait; Jessica was the one who needed help.

Something hit him on the nose. Startled, he glanced up; it was beginning to rain. Damn. Things were working against him. He jogged down the hill back towards Jessica's garden. It was after ten. The past four hours had dragged interminably. Time for action.

He crouched down low against the back fence, until he reached the junction with Mr Reader's fence. He followed this, as a reddish tree, some apple trees and the shed supplied a natural screen. The rain was falling steadily now, and he decided to take shelter under the great, sweeping branches of the cedar. It was dry and safe under there, and the tree gave off a heady, pungent smell. He swung up onto the curving branch where he had watched Jessica once, and bounced gently up and down. Through a small slit in the foliage he had a clear view of the side door. There was no sign of life.

It was so comfortable on the branch. Nice to just lie back and swing; worry about nothing. He began to feel a sneaking regret about the whole thing. If he ran home now, perhaps . . .

Ashamed, he jumped down. How could he have forgotten that Jessica was trapped inside, perhaps badly hurt. Allowing himself no more time to brood he streaked across the grass to the side door and tried the handle. It opened at once. He shut it softly behind him and leaned against the door, breathing hard. He was in a tiled passageway, dark, cool and uncluttered. There was no sound but the beating of his own heart and his light, quick breathing. He swallowed, then crept along the passageway, one hand trailing against the wall. He passed an open door on his right — some sort of storeroom. Then a door on his left, slightly ajar. Cautiously he slid it further open and peered round: the kitchen. Two more doors, one on either side, both closed. Probably cupboards, larders, that sort of thing. Then a swing door; it creaked a little as he pushed it open, and he stood motionless, ready to fly back the way he'd come. But there was no other sound. He was now in a large, partly tiled, partly carpeted hall, with four doors leading off it, in addition to the swing door, and a wide staircase on the nearer side. If Jessica was badly hurt, she would be upstairs in one of the bedrooms; if not, then she would be working somewhere, and he should be able to hear the clatter of her dustpan and brush. He decided to try upstairs first.

He was just setting a foot on the bottom stair when he heard something to his left. He shot round the bottom of the staircase and dived among some coats which were hanging from hooks along the side of the hall.

A shuffling step on the tiled floor and the sharp tap of a stick. Sam prayed that she would not choose a door at his end of the hallway; he was sure that the coats did not completely conceal him. To his relief, the tapping stick crossed the hall, and he heard the squeak of the swing door as it closed behind her. Now was his chance.

He raced up the stairs, two at a time, and stopped, undecided, at the top of the first flight. Was Jessica's room more likely to be on this floor or the next? The attic seemed more probable.

These stairs were not carpeted like the first, and his bounding steps thudded like gunshot. Bare boards along a corridor, dust, and no sounds but those his own feet made.

There were two doors on either side of the corridor. He was about to try the first when he heard a slight noise. He turned, startled, and crept back towards the staircase. Standing at the bottom of the second flight, her hand resting on the stair-rail, was Jessica. Her pale face was upturned to his. There was a large, padded plaster on her forehead. She was wearing a long, high-necked nightgown. The left sleeve was rolled up and Sam could see that the arm was bandaged.

Face to face with her at last, Sam was tongue-tied.

They stood motionless, staring at one another open-mouthed. open-mouthed.

"Who are you?" she said at last. She had a soft, clear voice and rolled her r's. "What are you doing here?" Then, drawing back from the stairhead, her body tensed as if ready to dart away, "You're not a thief, are you?"

He winced and stepped back.

Cautiously, she replaced her hand on the stair-rail, her eyes unwaveringly upon him.

Pulling himself together, he stepped forward. "Of course I'm not a thief," he hissed.

"Have you come to clear out the attic?" she asked. Then, frowning, "I didn't hear the doorbell."

He was non-plussed. How to explain his presence without alarming her?

"I think," she said imperiously, "you'd better come downstairs with me and explain yourself."

"No," he said, alarmed. "No. You mustn't do that!"

"So you *are* a thief," she accused. She backed away across the landing to the first flight of stairs, still watching him carefully. "I'm going to call —."

"Please. Don't!"

The two short words, whispered, held a real note of desperation. The girl hesitated.

Sam saw his chance. "I'm not a thief," he whispered urgently. "Cut my throat and hope to die. But I've got to talk to you."

She looked puzzled. "Why me? I don't even know you."

"But *I* know *you*." Her eyes widened with surprise — or

alarm? "I've seen you, often. Please, come up here — quick — and I'll explain."

Her frank, unblinking gaze was disconcerting. "I don't know," she said, half to herself, "if I should."

"I won't hurt you," he promised, "and I haven't done anything wrong. Honestly."

He was a thin boy with a pale skin. His eyes were large, dark and expressive. He didn't look particularly shabby or poor, not like a desperate character, and his voice and eyes held a real appeal. She judged that he was about her size — perhaps not so tall — and his hands were empty. No weapon.

"All right," she said at last.

Keeping her eyes firmly on him, she slowly climbed the stairs, sliding her right hand along the wooden banister rail.

They stared at one another curiously. Her eyes were a brilliant blue — not grey, as he had imagined — and almond-shaped.

Sam was afraid of losing the initiative. "In here." He grabbed the handle of the first door on the right.

She laughed. Laughed?

Sam hesitated and turned his head. "What's funny?" he asked warily.

"It might be a bit of a squash," she said. "That's the broom cupboard."

He glowered at her, and tried the next door. It opened on to a small room, empty apart from a couple of upright chairs — one broken — and some tea chests. It was thick with dust and had a musty smell. Jessica followed him and stood just inside the door, ready to run if necessary.

"Close the door."

She raised her chin in a small gesture of defiance. "I'd rather leave it open," she said.

They watched each other cautiously, and Sam, who was painfully aware that he was the shorter of the two, drew himself up to his full height.

"I know more about you than you think," he announced. "I know why you're bandaged up . . ."

"How?" she interrupted.

"Look. I'll explain later. I'm your friend. Trust me. The first thing is to get away. Then —."

"Get away?" Her mouth and eyes widened in surprise.

"You can't stay," he said. "I think you're very brave. But now's your chance."

Her face was troubled. "I don't understand. How do you know?"

"I've *seen* things. You wouldn't believe what things I've seen!" His eyes glowed.

She believed he had. He spoke with such conviction. "What sort of things?" she asked breathlessly.

"An old man in a rainbow-coloured helmet — clothes dancing — bullying and beatings, and fire —."

"Where did you see them?" she interrupted eagerly. "When?"

"From a window — high, high up."

She edged further into the room. "Tell me more."

He sat back on his heels. "I've seen a girl with golden hair dragged to a dark place and locked in there, all alone. I saw a great, hungry fire, and the golden girl fought it single-handed . . ."

Jessica crouched down beside him, listening intently.

". . . she would have put it out, I know, but the old woman and the Dark Lady fell upon her and . . ."

"J. J.!"

Sam's sharp ears caught the high-pitched sound. His head jerked up. His eyes cleared, and he leapt towards the door. "What was that?"

"Where are you, you little minx?" The voice was thin and quavery.

"It's *her*!" he hissed. "She mustn't find me here. You'd better go and see what she wants."

Jessica dreamily stood up and walked slowly to the door. As she slid past him, he caught her by her good arm. "You won't tell her I'm here?"

The sudden contact jolted her back to the reality of the situation. She shook off his hand. "Why shouldn't I? If you've got a good reason for being here I don't see why —."

"I'm in trouble," Sam pleaded. He racked his brains for some suitable explanation. If he lost her now, there might never be another opportunity.

"J. J!" The reedy voice rose to the attic like a thin spiral of smoke.

"I've run away from home," he said. "You can help me. Please believe me."

"All right," she said slowly. "I won't tell."

Sam was thinking hard. "Listen," he said urgently. "Is there any time when she's likely to be out of the way?"

"Out of the way?"

"Does she rest, or anything?" Sam was all impatience.

"No." She started to back out of the room. "Listen, I must go. I'm supposed to be in bed."

Sam leapt forward. "Wait!"

"It's okay." She eyed him steadily. "I won't tell. You stay here; she never comes up here. I'll find you later — when I can."

She slipped out so quietly, in her bare feet, that Sam almost questioned whether she had actually appeared. Her pale hair, skin, and nightdress — her soft voice and silent feet. She might have been a spectre.

Impatiently, he shook his head like a dog trying to shake water. Of course she was real. She was Jessica — Jessica of the laundry, the shed, the cedar tree. Jessica the Persecuted —

hadn't she got plasters and a bandage to prove it? He had seen her stagger under the rain of blows.

But could he be sure of her? Surely, whether she believed him or not, she wouldn't rat on him.

Why had she seemed so startled — frightened even — when he'd told her that he knew about her? Could it be that the aunt had a hold on her? It had puzzled Sam that the girl had put up with so much; Mr Forbes had found it odd too. Could it be that she, too, had a dark secret? He couldn't believe that she would deliberately do anything really wrong, but perhaps she had unintentionally caused some disaster. Maybe that was why he felt so drawn to her. They were two of a kind.

"I will help you," he resolved.

After Mrs Hooper left, Sophie Leonard was overwhelmed by paralysis. Her lonely, disturbed son had gone — she didn't know where, or when. He had no one to turn to.

The only people she herself could turn to were the authorities, in one form or another. She had already rejected the idea of informing the police. Mrs Hooper and Mrs Ellington worked for the educational section of the local council. They were good people, trustworthy, concerned for Sam's welfare, but they were in part responsible for Sam's disappearance. In their desire to help they had hemmed him in and made him panic. So she reasoned, as she stood irresolutely in the hall.

What she could not admit was that her inactivity was a product of her own guilt. She had been inadequate; she had tried to hide from her own grief, becoming a sort of refugee, and dragging her son into the camp with her. She had failed him when he most needed her, and now he had rejected her.

Time ticked by as she sometimes stood, sometimes paced, in the little hall. When at last, with a sort of shudder, she acknowledged to herself that she must *do* something, her first positive action was to look at her watch. It was 11.45.

Exclaiming at her own ineptitude she began to rummage feverishly in the coat rack, until she realized that she was wearing her mac. She must have put it on when she ran to the shops first thing in the morning, and had not removed it. She grabbed her bag and hurried out of the flat.

It was raining steadily. Sometimes jogging, sometimes running, until forced to a walk by shortness of breath, she hunted about the town. She scoured the park, the cafés, small open spaces, bus shelters. Went in and out of shops, hunted through the library, bought a viewer's ticket for the swimming bath and searched the water for a sign of Sam. She went to the railway station and the bus depot, asking anyone she saw there if they had seen a boy of such a height and age, with hair and eyes of just this shade, wearing sneakers and anorak which she described almost to the smallest stitch. She walked to the cinema to check the programme times but, being a weekday, and too early, it was locked up. Nowhere was there any sign of Sam.

At last, exhausted, she returned to the flat. Mr Forbes, it seemed, was her last chance. If he would not speak with her, then she would go to him. She looked up his address in the directory and, taking down the box containing his letters, she again let herself out of the flat.

Thirteen

When Mr Forbes' stomach started rumbling, he became aware of the fact that he was peckish. It was only then that he glanced at his watch to discover that it was nearly two. Two o'clock, and Mrs Butts had brought him no lunch! He leaned over the side of the bed, picked up his stick, and beat it upon the floor. Usually, this brought Mrs Butts to his bedside fairly promptly, but on this occasion it had no such effect. He thumped again, and then sank peevishly back on his pillows.

It did not occur to him to bestir himself, and fetch something from the kitchen. After all, his midday meal was a simple affair, as he had instructed; an apple, some bread and cheese, and a pot of tea. Instead, he wasted a good deal of breath roundly cursing his housekeeper, and then cheered himself with the prospect of dinner at seven. It would taste all the better for the fast, and Mrs Butts was a good cook. Sighing a little petulantly, he picked up his book again.

He read on undisturbed until his ears pricked up at the squeak of the thirteenth stair. Ah, supper! But his watch read 3.10. He shook it impatiently and put it to his ear. It was still ticking.

The bedroom door opened, and the space was filled by Mrs Butts.

He raised his eyebrows enquiringly.

"The lady's come to see you," she said.

"What lady?"

"The lady as has lost her son. Her that telephoned."

"I've told you already, Mrs Butts," cried Mr Forbes shrilly, "that her carelessness is no affair of mine. And where's my —?"

"Very good, sir," said Mrs Butts impassively. She withdrew and closed the door.

Down in the hall she looked kindly at the pale, distressed lady. "He'll come round," she said. "You'll see."

The lady wrung her hands. "But it may be too late. I've wasted so much time."

Mrs Butts nodded. "Come and sit by the Aga," she said. "It's warm there and you look freezed up. I'll make you a cup of tea. Then," she said firmly, before the lady could interrupt, "I'll work on him."

Obediently Mrs Leonard followed the woman who, though she looked awesome, was clearly an ally. She was sat upon a wooden chair up against the Aga, which was indeed warm and comforting. The steam from her drenched clothes soon merged with that from a large striped mug of tea which was placed in her hands.

"I won't be long," said the woman with a brusque nod, and she vanished up the ill-lit corridor.

The thirteenth stair squeaked again, and Mr Forbes cocked his head. He forebore to look at his watch this time.

"She'll not go till she's seen you," stated Mrs Butts, marching right up to his bedside. "And you'll get no dinner till you've spoken with her."

Mr Forbes stared at her. "No dinner? But you haven't given me lunch."

She stood in silence, arms akimbo, looking like some great monument carved out of stone.

"You are being most unreasonable." His voice was plaintive, and his thin hands moved restlessly over the coverlet. His stomach rumbled noisily, and he felt the onset of the cramps that had always afflicted him if he did not feed regularly. "A little, and often," he remembered his sister Ethel saying.

"Different people have different needs, but you need small meals at regular intervals. You've got an acid stomach."

"I don't know as who's being unreasonable," volunteered Mrs Butts.

"But I've *told* you," he protested. "I don't know the woman. How can *I* be expected to help her?"

"Those as don't try, can't find out,' retorted Mrs Butts.

Mr Forbes strained forward and pointed an angry finger at his housekeeper. "How dare you!" he cried. "Your place is in the kitchen, preparing my meals and keeping my house."

"I know my place," she replied stolidly.

"You're sacked!" growled her employer.

"Then you'll get no dinner no ways. You see the lady first, then we'll see whether I goes or not."

Mr Forbes peered perplexedly at her. Her mouth was set. She meant business. It was the woman and dinner, or no woman, no dinner.

"All right," he submitted petulantly.

Having got dressed and gone downstairs, he found the two women in the back room, where he used to read before he retired to bed. Mrs Butts promptly stationed herself by the door and there stood sentinel.

The woman who was responsible for disrupting his day was sitting stiffly in *his* chair. She was pale-skinned and petite, with dark, curling hair. Had he been feeling more generous toward her he might even have grudgingly admitted that she was rather pretty.

She leapt up at his entry and fixed huge eyes on him. "Do you know where Sam has gone?"

"I don't know who Sam is," he growled. "Never met the fellow."

"But you corresponded with him!" She turned, and picked up a cardboard shoe-box from the arm of the chair. She held it out to him. "Here," she said, shaking the box. "They're all in here. Your letters and the advertisement."

He peered into the box doubtfully; all he could see was a blue exercise book. "What letters?"

She glanced down, saw the exercise book — which she did not recall being there before — and shoved it into the old man's hands. Then she drew out the letters and thrust them at him. "Here. Here," she said.

Awkwardly clutching the bundle, he backed to a chair and began to inspect them. He recognized the letters at once; they were indeed his. "Well, why didn't you *say*," he grumbled. "These are my letters to S.L." His eyes lit again upon the exercise book, which he opened. The handwritten pages were difficult to read but he saw enough to realize that here were the author's original jottings. Here was Jessica, the terrible aunt, Mr Reader. He glanced up, delighted. "These are my stories," he said triumphantly.

"*Your* stories? Let me see them." Mrs Leonard snatched the book from him and began to read. So Sam's stories had been at home all the time, and he had never shown them to her. As she read, she began to realize why. These were not like any stories he had written before; they were strange, at times frightening. She was appalled. Her Sam had written these? Where had he unearthed this strange world? And yet there were points in the stories where she had an odd sense of familiarity. The description of the two houses on the moor — where had she seen houses like that? The account of Mr Reader popping out between the gate posts with a book under his arm. The overgrown garden with the cedar tree. The nightmare — yes, Sam had had nightmares like that. The final pages vividly described a fire.

Closing the book, she looked wonderingly at the old man. "Are these the stories my son sent you?"

"Yes." He grinned. "They're good, aren't they? Can't spell, too many adjectives, but —."

She stared at him, seeing him clearly for the first time. "I've met you somewhere before," she said.

"No, you have not," replied Mr Forbes. He turned to Mrs Butts. "Did you say he's gone away? Well, we must find him! We must track him down and get him writing again. Perhaps he's had a brainstorm. Writers do, you know."

Sophie Leonard was staring still at the old man. So cool and sure. Not a pathetic little old pensioner at all. She trembled with indignation.

"How dare you!" she stuttered. "How dare you assume —. Filling my son's head with silly notions. Calling him an author. Those stupid letters! How could you be so irresponsible!" She thumped her fists on the arms of his chair. "He had enough to cope with — we both did — without this. It's your fault," she cried, "that he's run away. Giving him all that money. Giving him ideas."

She clasped her hands together and shook them under his nose. "It's your fault you — you — silly old man!"

Always prone to cry when angry, she licked her salty top lip and rapidly blinked to try and disperse the give-away tears.

Held captive in his chair, since he could only rise from it by removing Mrs Leonard first, Mr Forbes cried, "Well! I'll be damned! *My* fault, is it?" They glared at each other.

"He's a *boy*. An unhappy, confused little boy!"

"A boy? How was *I* to know he was only a boy?"

"You should have known," she accused. "Anyone else would."

He sucked in his bottom lip. This was all most disconcerting.

Still leaning over him, "I know," she said slowly. "I know where I've seen you before. Through Sam's binoculars — on the hill. He showed me. And the houses, they're the houses on the hill. *Your* house . . . . What have you been doing to him?"

She drew back and nervously ran her fingers through her hair. "The stories have something to do with it," she said distractedly. "But what of the girl? And the deformed old woman? And the fire in the garden?"

Mrs Butts had said nothing throughout the exchange. She had not the least idea what either of them was talking about. But "the fire in the garden" she did know something of.

"Well, that's rare," she exclaimed. "There was a fire next door only last night. I saw the flames from my kitchen window. That poor child, fighting all on her own to put it out. I got him" — she nodded curtly at Mr Forbes — "out of bed, and we ran round to help. We put it out, but the little girl was burned, poor thing."

Sophie Leonard took Mrs Butts by the forearms. "Who lives next door?" she asked breathlessly.

"There's an old lady — Mrs Coutts — who has a twisted mouth — the devil's mark my mother used to call it — though she's a pleasant enough lady; and a young girl — her granddaughter, I believe."

Mrs Leonard stared at her thoughtfully for a moment, then made for the door. "I think I begin to see. We must go there at once." She hurried down the corridor.

"I'll come with you, Mrs. Mrs Coutts knows me," Mrs Butts called after her.

Mr Forbes sat in his chair, feeling dazed and rather old. Then, with a grunt and a wheeze, he levered himself upright and made for the door. "These foolish women are all over the place," he complained.

Fourteen

Sam tried not to pace about the uncarpeted attic, for fear of his steps being heard by Jessica's aunt. But it was difficult to keep still. Time in this echoing, musty place seemed to drag backwards. He felt incapable of forming a plan. He had nothing to eat; his haversack was in the garden, hidden in the bush. He wondered whether he should creep down to the first floor and hunt out Jessica's bedroom, but he was afraid to. This waiting had eroded his courage.

But she had promised to come to him when she could. Resigned to that, he at last settled himself on the floor in a corner of the room with the two chairs, his back against the wall.

He woke to find Jessica shaking his shoulder, and glanced up at her fearfully. "What is it?"

"I've brought you this." Shyly, she held out a roll. "I guess you're hungry."

Gratefully, he bit into it. It was good, and filled generously with ham and tomato. "Thanks," he spluttered through a mouthful.

She was smiling. It was a wide, sweet smile. "Is that better?" she enquired solicitously, tilting her head to one side.

Sam nodded, and wiped his mouth with the back of his hand. He felt awkward, and simply didn't know what to do next.

He need not have worried. Jessica had her own ideas.

"You can't run away," she said. "How would you live?"

He was puzzled for a moment. *He* wasn't running away,

was he? Then he remembered that he had given this as his explanation for being in the house.

"Is it that awful?" she asked. She sat back on her haunches and considered him solemnly. "Do your parents beat you up?"

"No!" he cried indignantly.

"Then why have you run away?"

Her persistence was unnerving. Sam realized he must put things right. "I've only run away — for a bit," he said. "I've come to help *you*. You're the one who must run away. I've brought money," he added hastily, as her mouth dropped open. "Quite a lot, actually."

Kneeling on the dusty floor, she stared at him. She said slowly, "But I don't want to run away."

It was Sam's turn to stare. How could she not grasp this opportunity? Anything must be better than the life she led now. And she had an ally, someone who would help her all he could. All his hopes and fears were concentrated upon her release.

He grasped her by the shoulders. "You must!" he insisted through clenched teeth. "You've got to escape now. You'll never have another chance."

The boy's face was close to hers. His brooding eyes were wide and desperate. What sort of a boy was he? One moment he seemed gentle and appealing; the next, fierce and persistent. Was he perhaps a little mad?

"You've got to! You've got to!" he cried. In his anxiety, he clutched at her bandaged arm.

She let out a little, high wail and, frightened, he let go of her. "What is it?"

"You've hurt my arm," she whispered. Her eyes were filmed with tears.

"I'm sorry. I didn't mean to hurt you." He drew back, appalled. "But don't you see? I'm your friend. There's no need to be scared. I've watched you for weeks through my binoculars. I sort of understand what it feels like to be a prisoner — I've been one myself. I don't know what you've done wrong — what she's got on you — but I'm sure it wasn't your fault. Any more than —." He paused and grimaced. "Any more than my dad's death was really my fault."

"You're stupid, or crazy, or both," she announced defiantly, nursing her arm. "I'm not a prisoner, and I haven't done anything wrong. *You're* the one who's in trouble."

He leant forward on his hands and glared at her. "That's what *you* think! You're a coward, that's what you are. Afraid to admit — whatever it is. Scared of that old crone. You're just a funk!"

"I'm not scared of anything — least of all you. And don't you dare call my grandmother 'that old crone.' " Frightened and hurt — for she had chosen to trust and help this boy who had responded with nothing but insults — she was determined not to give her feelings away.

"Your grandmother? She's your grandmother?"

"Of course she is. I care about her. She can't help looking funny."

"You *like* her? How can you like her when she's so cruel? You can't fool me. I know how you got that plaster and bandage."

"Oh, you do, do you? Well, actually, I got burned in this fire. If it hadn't been for my grandmother I might've been much worse hurt. She wouldn't hurt me." Indignation dispelled her fear. "Just because she's got a hare lip doesn't mean she's a wicked old witch."

"Hare lip? What's that?"

"You're ignorant, too. It's something you're born with, that makes your mouth all crooked. But she's clever. She used to be a teacher. She's helping me study for my entrance exam to a boarding school. My dad gets sent all over the place with his work and I kept changing schools. They decided to send me here to catch up. I bet my gran could teach *you* a thing or two."

Sam stared at her, uncomprehending. "You *like* her, your aunt? I mean, grandmother? You really like her, Jessica?"

"Of course I do. And my name isn't Jessica. It's Jane."

Sam felt as if the room was receding, leaving him in a great, empty space.

Jane's anger increased as the boy's confidence waned. "Seems to me," she said deliberately, "that you've got a lot of things wrong. I don't believe about your dad, or anything. You've just made it up, like you invented a name for me, and an evil old aunt keeping me prisoner." She looked at him challengingly.

His face, naturally pale, had turned chalky. The huge, brooding eyes began to moisten, seemed to swell. He blinked fast and turned his head away.

"He is dead," he said slowly. "And I killed him." He drew his knees up to his chin and tightly encircled them with his arms.

With face averted, he began to rock gently.

How strange he was; so many wild stories. Perhaps he wasn't crazy, after all; just confused and unhappy. Jane's anger died as suddenly as it had flared. Instinctively, she extended a reassuring hand to him.

He flinched, then cried out as if she had hit him. Jumping up, he ran out of the room and down the stairs, making no effort to conceal himself. He must get away — get away.

Distantly he heard her calling him, but that just drove him on.

"Wait!" Jane called. "Oh, please don't run away! I didn't mean to . . . "

She ran to the top of the staircase but he had gone. She ran back to the little room and pressed her face against the cold window pane. She didn't notice that the sky had cleared; that the trees were awash with sunlight. She saw only an empty, sodden garden. Then she tensed, for across the grass the boy careered, stumbling as if half blind. He ran past the vegetable patch and crashed into the shrubbery along the back.

She sighed with relief. "He's gone that way." Turning from the window, she noticed a pair of binoculars upon the floor. He had said that he saw her often through binoculars. She picked them up, then sped barefoot to her bedroom, threw off her nightclothes and began to dress.

Crying hysterically as he pounded up the hill, Sam fought for breath. When he broke free of the woodland and came out on the moor, he was forced to stop. His chest hurt dreadfully, and his heart seemed lodged in his ears, banging like a tom-tom. He bent double to try and ease the pain.

Thoughts crashed about in his head like breaking glass. She doesn't believe me. Her aunt is a granny. Her grandmother's nice. She's running — no — I — I'm running. Away. Mummy. He's dead. Daddy *is* dead.

Jane found him still bent double. Too breathless herself to speak, she also touched her toes to relieve a sharp stitch.

At last she straightened up. "Here," she said, holding out the binoculars. "You left them behind." He took them silently and strung them round his neck.

"I'm sorry," she said. "I didn't mean to upset you. You didn't kill your dad. Of course you didn't."

He said nothing for a moment, but stood with his chin sunk on his chest; when he spoke his voice was muffled. "I free-wheeled down the hill. I wasn't supposed to. To meet my dad at the junction. The brakes wouldn't work. He said I should check them but I didn't. He trusted me."

"Then what happened?"

"I don't remember."

"Yes. You do." She regarded him anxiously. "You do remember. But you can't stand to."

Sam felt small and lost. The grass, his hands, her shoes were all a blur. He closed his eyes tight and frowned with concentration. What *had* in fact happened? What *could* he remember? It seemed immensely important that he should get it right; that she should understand exactly what happened.

He spoke haltingly, dredging up images as they came to him. "I saw this Roots van driving across. Then I saw Daddy. He was running towards me, yelling. He must have guessed I couldn't stop. He ran into the road, and he grabbed my bike. He was knocked down by a car — a red car, I think."

"And he was killed? Saving you?"

Sam nodded.

"Ohhh," she sighed. Then, gently, "What's your name?"

"Sam."

"That's awful, Sam. Oh, but it wasn't your fault."

He raised his head and blinked at her. "Wasn't it?" he pleaded.

"No." She shook her head vehemently. "It was an accident."

Awkwardly they faced each other. She raised her right hand and said, "Like this."

He rubbed his eyes with his fists and saw that her index finger was bent at the second joint. "How did you do that?"

"Mummy slammed it in the car door."

"It must have hurt," he said.

"It did."

There was an uncomfortable silence.

Jane fidgeted a little, then looked about her. "It's nice here," she said. "I haven't been up here before. I haven't been anywhere since I came to Grandmother's. Just work, work." She turned back to Sam who was watching her intently. "I want to catch up on all the things I've missed. I'd love to play up here," she said wistfully, "with a friend."

"It would be nice," Sam replied.

Jane smiled at him shyly. She tossed her head, so that her long hair danced. "Let's race!" she cried. She began to run, stumbling across the tussocky grass and heather. Sam hesitated, then broke into a trot.

Fifteen

Mrs Leonard hurried up the front path of the big house next door and rang the doorbell. Several minutes' wait produced no response, so she pressed again. She saw a shadow through the coloured glass in the door, and a moment later it opened. An elderly lady in rather eccentric clothes stood bent in the doorway. Her hands were severely twisted with arthritis, and her hare lip gave her wrinkled face a lop-sided appearance. But her light eyes were bright. Mrs Leonard recognized her at once as the cruel aunt in Sam's story.

"Yes?" she enquired, frowning slightly. Then she smiled. It was an ugly smile, since it twisted her mouth still more, but her eyes curled into a network of laughter lines at the corners.

"Of course," she said, looking over Mrs Leonard's shoulder at Mrs Butts. "You're my kind neighbour. I was just this minute writing to thank you for your help with the fire last night. Such a fright it gave us all. My granddaughter is not too badly burned, thank goodness, and the doctor soon calmed her down. I'm sure she'd like to thank you herself. Please, do come in."

They followed her into a spacious, tiled hall. "Jane," she called. "J. J. Someone's called to see you, dear." She began to walk towards the staircase.

Sophie Leonard took advantage of the moment's silence. "We've come about my son," she said. "Has he called here? Sam Leonard?"

Mrs Coutts turned at the foot of the stairs. "Boy? I know of no boy. My granddaughter is the only child here."

"Are you sure? You see he —."

"Quite sure. Jane!" she called up the stairs. "Perhaps she's asleep," she explained. "She had a nasty shock. I'll go and check." Slowly she ascended the stairs with the aid of her stick.

"Oh, this is intolerable!" cried Mrs Leonard.

Mrs Coutts paused in her tortuous ascent, and looked down.

"I'll help you," cried Mrs Leonard, leaping up the stairs.

"But I don't think that will be . . . ." The old lady, much startled, stared after the strange woman who bounded up the staircase two stairs at a time and disappeared along the first-floor corridor, calling "Sam! Sam!" as she ran.

Mrs Coutts looked to Mrs Butts for an explanation. "I don't understand," she complained. "Who is she? And who is Sam? Is she demented?"

Mrs Butts joined her. "She's very upset, Mrs Coutts," she explained. "She's lost her boy, Sam, and she thinks he might be here, with your granddaughter."

Mrs Coutts shook her head. "But Jane doesn't know any children. She won't find him here."

"Maybe you're right," said Mrs Butts soothingly, and she began to steer the elderly lady up the stairs.

Though Mrs Coutts suffered herself to be led up her own staircase, she was far from reassured. "This is all most disturbing," she said, shaking her head from side to side. "I still don't see why your friend should think her son is here. You know my granddaughter has had a shock. She must not be alarmed."

In their slow progress they had just attained the first landing when Mrs Leonard reappeared.

"He's not here!" she cried. "Neither of them are. We must look downstairs."

Mrs Coutts said anxiously, "But Jane is in her bedroom."

She was not, however. Her night things were strewn on the floor, and her drawers were untidily open, with clothes hanging out as if she had dressed in a hurry.

"Where is she?" The old lady pressed her hands to her cheeks. "Where has Jane gone?" Then, "Of course," she reasoned, "she must be in the garden, the naughty girl."

The doorbell rang. "I'll get it," said Mrs Butts.

Mrs Leonard beat her to the front door. Her face fell when she found Mr Forbes on the doorstep.

"Oh it's you," she said rudely. "They must have gone out." She pushed past him into the front garden.

Mrs Butts glared at her employer, and rejoined Mrs Coutts who was tapping across the tiled hallway.

"She's sure to be in the garden," repeated the old lady, and the two women slowly followed Mrs Leonard.

"Haven't they found him yet?" grumbled Mr Forbes. "I should like a word with that young man." He, too, made for the garden, closing the front door behind him.

They could hear Mrs Leonard calling Sam from somewhere round the back of the house.

"Jane!" called Mrs Coutts. "Jane!"

Mr Forbes appeared, and began rooting around in the vicinity of the garden shed.

Mrs Butts found the sight of three adults — two of them decidedly elderly — poking around in a town garden faintly ridiculous. If they *was* here, she thought, they would give themselves up. Ironically, it was she who found the clue. Without much conviction, she had made her way to the shrubbery at the back of the garden, where she noticed that a branch of a spreading rhododendron was snapped. Leaning forward to break the offending branch at the split, her eye caught something yellow on the ground further in the bush. Muttering a little, for the bush was spiky and brittle and she was no sylph, she pushed her way in and stooped to pick the object up. It was a grubby yellow towel. She backed out of the bush and waved the towel like a flag.

"I've found something," she shouted.

Mrs Leonard was also at the end of the garden. She ran up to Mrs Butts. "What?" She snatched the soggy towel out of Mrs Butts' hand and examined it. "Where did you find it?"

Mrs Butts indicated the bush, and she at once pushed her way in among the twisted branches. She found Sam's haversack and, clutching it to her chest, backed out again. "It's his," she gasped, half-sobbing with relief. "He *has* been here. They can't be far away."

"The ground's wet," observed Mrs Butts. "We'll maybe find their footprints." They began to search in among the bushes, and Mrs Leonard soon found the gap in the fence. The bare earth on the garden side bore the distinct mark of smallish shoe prints, and the nettles and brambles on the further side had been trampled into a faint path. "They went that way," she said. She thrust Sam's haversack into Mrs Butts' arms, and squeezed through the gap.

"Where's *she* going?" enquired Mr Forbes, who had joined them.

"She's found her son's bag," explained Mrs Butts. "She thinks they've gone up the hill."

"Gone that way, have they, the scallywags," he grunted. He edged himself carefully through the gap and, thrusting his hands into his coat pockets, began to trudge up the hill in Mrs Leonard's wake.

"*I* don't know," mused Mrs Butts, who had no intention of trying to squeeze through that narrow space. Her sensible shoes were heavy with mud, and her stockings damp. She made her way cautiously out of the shrubbery and approached Mrs Coutts, who was hovering by the vegetable plot.

"This is very confusing. What is all this about?" wailed the distressed old lady. "Where is my granddaughter?"

Mrs Butts took her arm. "Not to worry, Mrs Coutts," she said reassuringly. "The two children have gone up the hill. They'll not have gone far. Mrs Leonard will bring them safe home, you'll see. *We* can't go climbing up hills now, can we? Let's warm ourselves with a pot of tea."

She firmly led the grandmother back into the house.

Brambles, birch and stunted oak gave way to tussock grass and gorse, and then she was out, clear, on an expanse of open heath. Mrs Leonard stopped to take stock. The children's trail had petered out some little way back, but the human figure should stand out clearly in this open terrain. She needed a high vantage point, and saw one in a slight rise to her left.

Standing on the knoll, she turned her head slowly, scanning the moor.

She was startled by the sound of girlish laughter quite close by. Turning towards the sound, she saw a figure rise up out of a patch of long grass about a hundred yards away. The girl's long hair looked white in the sunlight.

"What's that?" Her high voice carried clearly on the light breeze.

A second figure reared up out of the grass beside her. Both their faces were raised to the sky.

"A skylark, ignoramus."

"Where?"

The boy swivelled slowly, hands on hips and head thrown back. "There." He pointed to the sky, and put one arm around the girl's shoulder. "See that little black speck? That's it."

"I can't see anything."

"Here." He slipped his binoculars from his neck. "Try these." She took them awkwardly, and he steadied her hands with his own. His voice dropped to a murmur, and the onlooker could only guess that he was explaining how to use them.

The girl gave a delighted cry. "I see it!" She carefully lowered the binoculars. "It's not very pretty," she remarked. "But," she added hastily, "it sounds gorgeous."

He turned, then pointed across the grass. "And that's a rabbit," he solemnly informed her.

She nudged him and laughed. "I know *that*!"

The boy leapt, spun round and began to run towards the rise, his head swivelled back towards the girl. He shouted something, but the words were lost on the wind. Not looking where he was going he stumbled, righted himself, looked ahead, and stopped short so suddenly that the girl, running too, nearly collided with him.

"Mummy!"

She ran down the slope. "Sam! Thank God you're all right." She threw her arms around him. He wriggled free.

He grinned at her. "I'm okay, Mum."

Mrs Leonard stared at her son. First Mr Forbes, and now him. Did nobody understand what terrors she had experienced today?

She gripped his shoulders and shook him fiercely. "How dare you go off like that, without telling me? I've been worried sick. I didn't know where you were. What —."

His eyes, alight a moment earlier, clouded over. She could almost smell a sudden fear in him.

"I'm sorry, I'm sorry," he gulped. "I didn't think. I was so frightened for Jess — Jane. I thought she'd been beaten. I wanted to help her escape — with the money. I really thought she was in danger. But I got it all wrong. It was a mistake." His voice was rising to a pitch of hysteria. "It wasn't her, Mummy, she's all right. It was me. *I* was running away — from, from . . . "

Mrs Leonard suddenly held a mental picture of Sam as he had risen up out of the grass. She had seen, then, a normal boy, playing with a friend, absorbed and thoughtful, running on the moor.

She encircled him in her arms and this time he made no move to struggle free. "I know, darling. You've had a terrible time. But you're fighting like a man — like your dad would have done — to sort things out, and I'm proud of you. I'm really, really proud of you, Sam, and I'm so glad you're safe."

Over his head she saw the girl, standing a little way off with her head turned away.

"Jane," she called softly. The girl turned and looked at her shyly. She slowly approached mother and son.

"Would you like," asked Mrs Leonard, "to come and visit Sam sometimes? We could take trips to the countryside, bring a picnic."

Jane nodded. "Yes. I should like that." She glanced at Sam, whose head was still pressed against his mother's shoulder. "Sam says he'll teach me to fly a kite. We wondered . . . ." She hesitated, and looked hopefully at Mrs Leonard. "Sam says he's learning at home too. We thought maybe we could have lessons together. It would be more fun, wouldn't it?"

Sam's head stirred, and he raised a tearful and expectant face. "Could we, Mummy, please?"

She smiled. "Is that what you'd really like?"

"Yes." He nodded vigorously. "I'm sick of being on my own. I'd like to work with Jane." He paused, then added, "And she knows about Daddy. She says it was an accident."

"Of course it was an accident, Sam. Oh God, I didn't realize you still —."

"So this is the young author."

Startled, they turned to see the old man wheezing up the grassy slope.

Sam's eyes popped. "Mr Reader!" He glanced doubtfully at his mother. "His name's Mr Forbes," she said quietly.

With a final burst of effort, the old man topped the rise and stood before them.

"Well — young man —" he panted. "You should be ashamed of yourself. Leading us all such a dance. Deserve a good hiding —."

Jane stepped forward. "You are very unkind," she said. "He has been most upset."

The old man fixed the child with faded, wondering eyes. "Have I been unkind?" he enquired at last, gazing at her still. He turned to Sam. "Have I been unkind?"

"No, really, it's all right," Sam interposed hastily, colouring a little.

But Mr Forbes felt oddly ashamed. With his hands clasped in front of him, he stared uncomfortably at his feet. "I — I'm sorry, if that is the case," he said awkwardly. "I did not intend it."

Still holding Sam's shoulder, Mrs Leonard said, "We've all had a bit of a shock today. Jane's grandmother is worried. We must go back and reassure her." She smiled warmly at Jane, then, hesitantly, stretched out her free arm and took the old man's. "Come on."

The four made their way back down the hill, pacing themselves to the old man's slower tread. They topped the brow and paused, for a moment, as the houses on the hill came into view.